TAIL OF A FEATHER

THE SPELLWOOD WITCHES, BOOK 3

MELANIE SNOW

Spirit Paw Press, LLC

CONTENTS

The Spellwood Witches Series

Witch's Tail
Howl Play
Tail of a Feather
Impawsible Mischief
Pawtrayal

Tail of a Feather

The Spellwood Witches, Book 3

ASIN: B08K4S9D9T

ISBN: 978-1-7324375-8-6

(Spirit Paw Press, LLC, Concord, NH 03303)

www.wendyvandepoll.com/melanie-snow

Thank You

Download Your Free Gift

A Welcome to Witchland Map

Thank you for purchasing *Tail of a Feather, The Spellwood Witches, Book 3*. To show my appreciation and because of a popular request from my readers, I am offering a:

Welcome to Witchland Map

Just in case you forgot to download in Book 1, please download here.

https://wendyvandepoll.com/melaniesnowgift

Sarah snuggled into her jacket and relished the slight sting of the cold on the tip of her nose. Autumn was washing Witchland in rich oranges, browns, and yellows, and little frost crystals coated the ground in the morning. The scent of pumpkin pie and pumpkin spice espresso treats wafted continuously out of Javacadabra, where Susie and Karen worked tirelessly to delight the taste buds of the town with the help of their familiar, a talking white cat named Zeva.

Holding her tea latte between her palms to warm them, Sarah kept pace with Eli as they began the trek up the Mount Katribus trail. Sarah's canine familiar, Addie, padded along at her side. "I wonder why I love autumn so much." Sarah sighed contentedly.

"Because you're a witch," Eli teased, his gorgeous blue eyes twinkling as he smiled at her.

He wrapped his arm around her shoulders, and she snuggled in close. Addie looked up at them, love in her soft brown eyes. "*I must say your warmth for each other is keeping me warm,*" Addie joked.

Though Eli couldn't hear her, he was starting to get to know the loyal collie mix well, and he asked her, "Where is your boyfriend, Kelvin, huh, girl?"

Addie barked happily when she heard the name Kelvin. "*He's in the woods, hunting rabbits,*" she answered, which Sarah repeated to Eli so he could hear.

"Girls always love the bad boys. Or, in your case, the bad wolves," Eli said.

"So Jenna did the rounds this morning? There's no sign of Madras?" Sarah asked as the trail they were walking on began to incline up the mountainside. Eli Strongheart was the police chief of Witchland, and Jenna Mora was his deputy.

"Not a sign," Eli replied. "Tonight is my turn . . . I imagine these woods make you a bit nervous now, don't they?"

Sarah shrugged. "Not at all, actually. I love the woods so much that I won't let my wicked great-great-great-whatever-aunt ruin them for me. Besides, I feel so much more confident knowing that I defeated her. That she's banished for good."

Eli smiled. "We always try our best to keep these

woods safe. Even the greatest demon witch of all time can't defeat our team."

"So . . . I was thinking. I invited my parents to my house for a little dinner in two days. Would you like to join us?" Sarah went on. She had felt slightly apprehensive about inviting Eli, since they were a new couple. The last thing she wanted to do was scare him off. But she knew in her heart that Eli was in it for the long haul, and that made it easier to come out and say things, even things that made her nervous.

"Of course," Eli said, looking slightly taken aback. "Any weird quirks I should prepare for?"

"Um, definitely don't talk politics with my dad." Sarah laughed. "It could get pretty heated. Also, let's keep the magic talk to a minimum."

"I thought you told them that you're practicing witchcraft?" Eli said.

"I did. But it's a touchy subject. You know that my father tried so hard to put distance between himself and the Spellwood legacy." Sarah shrugged. "They're accepting, but I just don't want to make them super uncomfortable."

"I think you should just be yourself," Eli said gently. But then he added, "Although, I probably wouldn't talk about witchcraft to my mom, either. She's probably a far worse denier than your parents."

"Well, my parents don't deny it. They just don't

practice it. The last time was at my Aunt Beth's when we visited her, right before she passed away and I started seventh grade." Sarah suddenly stopped in the middle of the trail. Addie, who was wandering slightly ahead, turned back and looked at her expectantly. "Let's go visit Aunt Beth's. I haven't been able to bring myself to go since I moved here," said Sarah.

"Your Aunt Beth's house? Well, sure," Eli said, again taken aback. He laughed as they changed course and began to walk toward the small goat farm Beth Spellwood ran. "I love how spontaneous you are."

"I haven't seen her farm in so long, and I really miss that place. That was where I first discovered I had powers, and I was very close with my aunt." As Sarah attempted to remember her way through the maze of trails to the farm she had not visited since she was twelve, she regaled Eli with tales of Aunt Beth, including Aunt Beth's talking pet goat.

"So that was the original Addie," Eli commented.

"*Hey! No one is like me,*" Addie protested.

"That is true. You are one unique dog," Sarah assured Addie, who blinked at her happily.

They finally broke through the tree line and came upon a fence, which was sagging with the weight of the ivy growing on it. It enclosed a generous pasture with a goat shed in the center of it. Now, in place of the milk goats Aunt Beth had raised, there were two cows chewing cud listlessly. Beyond that, stood the modest farmhouse where Aunt Beth had lived, and where she and Sarah's father had grown up. Smoke curled from the chimney.

"So many memories." Sarah exhaled, feeling both joy and sorrow at the sight of her long-gone childhood. "I hope the family living here is happy."

"Too bad we can't go inside," Eli commented.

"I suppose we could always knock and ask." Sarah shrugged. She glanced at Eli, and when he agreed, she led him around the fence to the front door of the house. "Ah, I forgot about this knocker," she said, tracing the bronze gargoyle knocker with her fingertip after knocking. "I always thought it was so cool, but now I realize how out of place it was against this modest little house."

A woman carrying a baby on her hip opened the door. The minute she saw Sarah, her face softened in recognition. "You must be the little girl in all of those photos we found in the attic," she cried. "Beth Spellwood's niece?"

"Yes," Sarah said happily. "You found pictures?"

"Well, yes, we did, and we have them. We tried to send them to family, but we couldn't find an address. Come on in!" The woman stepped aside and ushered Sarah and Eli into the house. "Oh, hello," she greeted Addie, also welcoming her inside.

"Puppy!" several kids cried as they flocked around the dog. Addie rolled on the floor and showed her belly happily as the kids scratched it.

"My kids love dogs, as you can see." The woman laughed. "I'm Meg, by the way." She set the baby down and shook Eli's and Sarah's hands as they introduced themselves. Then she excused herself to retrieve the pictures. "You can take a look around, if you want," she called over her shoulder.

Sarah stepped into the kitchen. "The cauldron is gone." She sighed, noticing the open fireplace with its hanging cauldron was now replaced with an oven. The fridge was also new and covered in kids' art, with none of the strange recipes and spells that Aunt Beth kept on it.

Eli placed a comforting hand on her elbow. "You can't expect it to be the same."

"I know. It's just so different." Sarah sighed, breathing in the smell of the macaroni bubbling on the stove for lunch. "Well, actually, it seems like a happy home, and I'm just glad these people love it."

Meg reappeared with the photos. "Here you go!"

Sarah smiled as she sifted through them. "That was my goat!" she cried, showing Eli the photo of the black-and-white goat hanging his head over her shoulder.

"You were *cute*," Eli said. "So many freckles."

Teasingly, he touched her cheek, pretending to count the freckles she still had.

"She sure was," Meg said, nodding her head in agreement. Then she added in an undertone, "Do you want to go upstairs? I have to ask you about some things about this house . . ."

Sarah and Eli followed Meg up the narrow staircase to a landing. Meg paused in front of a door. "Um, I hate to mention this, but . . . I know the reputation of Lativia Spellwood."

Sarah smiled and nodded. "That is my ancestor, and the founder of Witchland." Then she narrowed her eyes knowingly. "Let me guess, weird things happen around this house?"

"Yes, well, Neil and I don't—well, we didn't believe in that stuff. Not at all. But after moving here . . ." Meg bit her lip, looking nervously from Sarah to Eli.

"We don't think you're crazy, don't worry," Sarah assured her. "Weird things happen in Witchland, and especially in this house. It did house three generations of witches." She and Eli exchanged knowing glances and then laughed, sharing memories of the many magical misadventures they had been on together in their efforts to protect Witchland from both Madras and greedy developers.

"Oh, good. I wasn't sure where you stood with all of that." Meg laughed nervously and gathered her hair into a ponytail. "Well, you see, we took the master bedroom here and . . ." She opened the door and pointed within.

Sarah stepped into her aunt's old bedroom. As if she were a child again, she could remember the four-post bed that took up most of the space, and the rolltop desk where Aunt Beth sat to pay her bills and write letters. Though the décor was different, the atmosphere of the room still felt like Aunt Beth: calm, sweet, earthy, loving. Tears welled up in Sarah's eyes.

"We keep cutting them back." Meg led them to the window, where several flowers emerged from the wooden frame, vibrant and colorful. They were growing without soil and without water. "We're not really sure how they keep growing."

Sarah touched one of the blue flowers gently. "My Aunt Beth loved her flowers, her garden, her goats. It was as if she was part of the natural world herself." She turned to Meg. "These are enchanted flowers that she grew because she thought they were pretty. The only way to remove them would be to break the enchantment."

"Oh." Meg looked worried. "I have no idea how to do that."

"I can bring some friends of mine by who can do that. If you don't mind, can I have them?" Sarah imagined planting them in her own room and always having a piece of Aunt Beth near her.

"Of course! I would hate to kill them, but it's just, well . . ." Meg shrugged haplessly. "Not our choice of décor. I hope that doesn't offend you."

"I get it." Sarah nodded. "It is your home now."

"Um, there's one other thing." Meg led them into the bathroom next and pointed to the blue tiles over the clawfoot bathtub, where Sarah had spent many afternoons pretending she was a mermaid in a frothy ocean of soap bubbles, with an army of rubber duckies to do her bidding.

Sarah smiled softly as she ran her fingers along the porcelain of the tub, entranced by her memories. Eli watched her, vicariously enjoying her reminiscing through the expressions on her face.

Meg turned on the shower. Gradually, words began to form across the tiles as the steam started to bloom from the water. Sarah squinted and realized that it was a spell for making the room smell like roses. Just as soon as she read the spell in her mind, the bathroom flooded with the flowery scent. "Aunt Beth's scent," Sarah murmured. "I always just thought it was a perfume."

"*It's strong, like Margaret and Hua's greenhouse,*" Addie complained, backing away toward the door.

"Any way you can break this enchantment? We love this scent, but . . ." Meg again looked hapless.

Sarah acquiesced and said a quick spell to erase the enchantment.

Spell be gone,
You have grown wan.
You have done well,
But it's no time to dwell.

Instantly, the words began to unfurl and stretch until they made a popping sound like bubbles and ran down the walls in streams of black ink. Then the ink grew clear and disappeared. The rose scent began to gently fade. *If only I could capture that scent in a bottle,* Sarah thought. *I have to enchant my bathroom to do that so that I can always smell Aunt Beth's rose scent.*

"I'm so sorry, and thank you so much," Meg said profusely as she showed them out. She handed Sarah the pictures in a bundle.

"Thank you for letting us inside and these pictures. I'll definitely treasure them. I'll come back with my friends, Margaret and Hua, later. They will transplant the flowers for you and remove the enchantment," Sarah promised.

As she, Eli, and Addie walked back into town,

Sarah sighed. "It's so hard to let go of the past and watch things change. I sure miss my aunt Beth."

"Can you visit her, you know, in that ghostly clearing?" Eli inquired. He was referring to the place where ghosts communed with Lativia Spellwood's ghost on the top of Mount Katribus.

"She moved on to the other side," Sarah said sadly. Then she interlaced her fingers with Eli's and cuddled against his muscular shoulder. "I miss her, but I know she's in a good place. And I'm very happy with how my life is now. I can only embrace the present."

Eli kissed the top of her head, and Sarah felt happy. "I think Aunt Beth would have adored you," she told Eli.

CHAPTER TWO

SARAH SAT ON HER ROCKER THAT EVENING, relishing the bright blue enchanted flowers now growing on pure air on her windowsill. "Someone will really wonder about that if I ever sell this place, just like Meg and her husband did in Aunt Beth's home," she said to Addie.

Addie lay at her feet, Kelvin the wolf stretched alongside her. She smiled lazily up at Sarah.

Sarah's phone dinged. She was glad to see Eli's name on the screen. "Just letting you know I'm starting my rounds in the forest," the text from him read.

"Okay, honey. Be careful," Sarah wrote back.

"I'll text when I'm back down the mountain," he responded. A second later, he sent another text: "I had such a good day with you."

"So did I!" Sarah smiled as she set the phone down.

Since her divorce from Jeff, her self-esteem and her belief in love had hit rock bottom. Eli was bringing both back up to soaring heights.

For the next several hours, Sarah finished some paperwork for a local case she was working on and read a cozy novel. Her eyelids grew heavy, but she fought sleep, waiting for Eli's text. Finally, she couldn't help it anymore and went to bed, where she fell into a deep sleep. Long hikes in the woods usually did that to her.

What on earth is all that noise? Sarah cracked her eyes open, disgruntled at being woken from her lovely dream of Eli feeding her tiramisu in a candlelit restaurant. The romantic violin serenade in her dream had been disrupted by the distinct sound of Addie barking fervently and—

"Are those crows cawing?" Sarah questioned while yawning and feeling bummed she was getting woken up.

Sarah's eyes flew wide open, and she turned her head to observe Addie standing before the bay window in the bedroom, wagging her tail and making enough noise to keep Sarah from falling off to sleep again. But Addie was not facing out the window; she was staring intently at Sarah, trying to wake her up.

"What is it, girl?" Sarah asked, swinging her legs out from under the cozy cover and shivering when her bare feet touched the cold floor. She located her slippers and strode up to the window. It let in only some feeble light, telling Sarah it was barely dawn. "It's *crazy* early. This had better be important," Sarah grumbled.

"The crows! They're telling us something!" Addie replied, jumping up and down in excitement now that she had successfully roused her person. *"They keep saying, 'Danger! Danger!'"*

Sarah rubbed the sleepy fog out of her eyes and stared down into the big maple tree that stood in front of her house. Its branches were heavily laden with shiny black crows, beaks open and wings flapping with the effort of their raucous chorus. While Sarah had often seen one or two crows in the woods and heard their croaks and caws, she had never seen such a large murder. The noise they were making was surely disturbing the entire town.

Addie barked. *"It's already six-thirty in the morning—and they say they just got here! For dog biscuits' sake, if they were ravens, they would have been here sooner. Can we call upon the ravens instead?"*

"What are they going on about?" Sarah demanded. "Why did they need to get here? Did they have an appointment?" She said the last part in jest. As a real estate attorney, she often received clients in the little front room of the cottage where she lived, though never this early and never of the feathered variety. She had inherited both the cottage and the law practice from her law school mentor and longtime friend, Michael Howler. In return, she had solved Michael's murder and brought justice and peace to his ghost, as well as the town of Witchland. Now, she lived here, carrying on Michael's law work for a living and protecting Witchland from evil the rest of the time.

"Sarah, you remember what Lativia, the greatest witch of all time, told us about seeing eight crows? Don't you?" Addie stared at Sarah intently with her large brown eyes, wagging her tail with expectation.

Sarah racked her brain. "She says so many things, and her messages are all insanely cryptic. I can't think right now, Addie."

"Your noble ancestor was extremely clear that they would be bearers of an important message and that they would signal bad news that you need to attend to," Addie said, a slight nip of impatience in her voice.

Sarah's eyes widened as the conversation with the ghost of her revered witch ancestor came back to her with vivid clarity. "Yes, of course. Now I remember she told us something about eight crows and about a slew of important questions, how they would be key to solving our next mystery in our town of Witchland," Sarah replied. She ran back toward her bed and scrambled around for her phone. "I need to see if Eli texted me back last night!"

"Well, I guess something bad happened last night and they just now got here," Addie said.

Just then, one of the crows flew onto the flower box in front of Sarah's living room windows and began to peck frantically at the glass. The loud tapping sound filled the house. The other crows began to caw even more loudly, and Sarah worried they were disturbing her neighbors, Margaret and Hua, who were always up this early tending to their massive greenhouse and many gardens. She became even more worried about something far more important when she noticed that Eli had not messaged her the night before. "That's not like him," she told Addie, her voice tight with anxiety.

"Let's go down there and see what the message is," Addie prompted. *"We can't waste a minute. It has to do with Eli; I can just tell by their caws."*

Panic gripped Sarah's chest. She hastily threw on her coat to guard against the autumn chill and chased her familiar outside. Her nose burned in the cold as she and Addie looked up toward the earsplitting sounds.

Within the branches of the maple tree sat seven crows. The eighth was perched on the branch closest to the front window, where it had been pecking to get their attention. Now, it turned from the glass and watched them with an intent stare, along with its cronies. With eight pairs of black eyes gawking down upon them, it was clear that the crows were dead serious about making contact with Sarah and Addie. Their already boisterous cawing intensified, and they began jumping around on the branches; the crows obviously had something quite urgent to say.

"*Quiet!*" barked Addie. "*One at a time. You all are hurting my sensitive ears. Let's get organized here.*" Despite her usual gentle nature, Addie's border collie side made her authoritative when she needed to be. Sarah always admired it when Addie broke out with her firmness.

"Tell me, what happened to Eli?" Sarah begged, wrapping her arms around her chest and bracing herself for bad news. After solving two murders in her six months in Witchland, she dreaded what the crows might tell her—but as an animal communicator, she knew she could trust what they had to say. *Do they even know how much Eli means to me?* she thought desperately.

"*You think we are going to just give you this information for free?*" said the largest crow. He stepped to the end of the branch closest to them, asserting himself as the leader. "*Since he is an integral part of Witchland's protection, we want to save Eli as well. But we are sick and tired of humans unfairly judging us. When people stop calling our family groups a murder—when, in fact, we are really a coven or clan that can offer the human race wisdom and guidance—we can then work together. Keep in mind, as is the case with wolves, we are intelligent, resourceful, and highly social creatures. Aligning us with such a heinous human misgiving as murder is highly insulting."*

"Seriously, I'm sorry everyone misunderstands you! But we can work on that later, don't you think? Please tell me—is Eli still alive? Is he all right?" sniffled Sarah. She had not even realized it, but now she was crying. Eli was the best thing to have happened to her in a long time, along with moving to Witchland and becoming reacquainted with her witch powers, which she had been repressing for all of her adult life.

Since her husband had left her and her boss had irked her to the point that she had quit her job, she had been rebuilding, growing, and becoming a complete person. It would be wrong to say she had become a new person—she had simply grown into her true self. But if she lost Eli, well, she had no idea what she would do.

"Do you know who sent us to you and why?" the crow asked instead of answering her question.

"Lativia told me you would show up when I needed you most for a very important case. And now you are here. I am truly grateful that you are helping us. I promise if we can work together to save Eli, I will do all I can to change how people treat you and what they call you. Tell me what to do and I will do it," Sarah beseeched them. "But we can do that later. Just tell me Eli is not dead!" The suspense had her heart thudding and her throat constricting; beads of cold sweat popped up along her brow.

"*Hmm. Let me talk with the rest of my coven,*" the leader crow said suspiciously.

"But there is no time for that," shouted Addie and Sarah in unison.

"*Yes, there is. Patience is one of the first lessons that we need to teach you. This will not take long,*" answered the crow.

"*Hurry,*" Addie growled. "*By the way, before you go, tell us your name.*"

"*Krell,*" squawked the head crow before he shambled deeper into the canopy of branches to confer with his sooty black cronies.

"*It can't be too, too serious, or they wouldn't be taking their time like this,*" Addie anxiously attempted to reassure Sarah. She always tried to make everything better, even if it meant she had to sacrifice her own comfort and happiness. That was why Sarah adored her so.

Sarah reached out to rub Addie's head affectionately. The smell of woodsmoke in someone's woodstove was crisp in the air, as well as the smell of the frost crackling under Sarah's boots. Sarah attempted to focus on those sensations instead of her intense worry and the gnawing feeling in her gut. "I certainly hope so," she mumbled.

On a sudden whim, she called Deputy Jenna Mora. "Have you heard from Eli since last night?" she demanded as soon as Jenna said hello.

"Uh, no," Jenna said. "You haven't heard from him?"

"Not a word, and he promised he would text me when he was finished with his rounds in the woods. But he didn't," Sarah cried.

"Oh my God. And you didn't think to look for him last night?" Jenna's irritation and fear were apparent in the tightness of her voice.

"I'm sorry! I fell asleep." Sarah already felt horrible for not waiting up for him. Maybe she could have averted disaster if she had been able to act faster.

"I'm coming right over," Jenna said hurriedly, hanging up.

Within a few minutes, Jenna came running up, out of breath and with her coat unbuttoned. "Okay, so he was in the woods, last you knew?"

"Yes." Sarah glanced up at the crows. Now they were silent and staring down at her, displeasure clear in their faces. "Sorry, guys, but I can't wait around for this. Eli's life is at stake. I can feel it in my bones. Jenna and I are going to search the woods for him."

Jenna peered at the tree and narrowed her eyes. "So the crows have something to do with it?"

"They won't really tell me. They just said they want to protect Eli, too, but they're wasting precious time," Sarah explained as she began walking to the woods.

"Yeah, sorry, crows, but we're not wasting time," Jenna told them flippantly.

The crows squawked with displeasure.

Jenna took the lead and showed Sarah the route she and Eli always took when doing their rounds. The route made the most efficient use of the trail system that cut through the Mount Katribus woods to cover the most ground. As they walked, Jenna attempted to call Eli on both his cell phone and his radio. "This isn't good at all," she remarked, as tense with worry as Sarah was.

"Last I heard from him was probably around eight," Sarah said.

Jenna checked her phone. "Yep, that's when I heard from him last, too." She then read aloud the message that Eli had also sent Sarah.

A tiny sting of jealousy entered Sarah's stomach that she was not the only recipient of his text before he left. But then she remembered he had said more about having a beautiful day with her. She knew that she was special to him, and she brushed the jealousy aside with an internal groan. *There's no need to be possessive of Eli. Jenna is just his deputy, even if she used to like him,* she thought.

"*You really are special to him,*" Addie assured her.

Sarah tried to smile, but her fear made it impossible.

Addie then put her nose to the ground and reported that she could still smell Eli's scent trail. They followed Addie, who said Eli had faithfully stuck to the trail route. After going up one side of the mountain and seeing no trace of Eli, they reached the top, the clearing where the ghosts communed.

Now, the clearing was oddly still, with none of its glowing blue residents drinking glowing blue wine from goblets and eating glowing blue food from a banquet table. Lativia and her throne were also not visible. Sarah realized the ghosts must be sleeping in whatever place they went to when they faded away. The trees stood mostly naked, and the floor was littered with leaves, relieving some of the gloom that usually shrouded the place. Since Sarah had never seen the clearing so deserted, it made her skin crawl. The silence was . . . too silent. Even without the evidence of its ghostly residents, Sarah could feel it was a highly spiritual place where the veil between the living and the dead was particularly thin.

"So this is the portal, created right where the Leekins banished Madras," Jenna commented, stopping before a place marked by two large mossy stones.

"Do you know where the portal goes?" Sarah glanced around, not seeing any signs of Eli whatsoever.

"No idea." Jenna exhaled loudly, then began gently lifting leaves on the path. "All I know is that it is somewhere far away from here, and I keep this portal sealed with spells." Then she paused and exclaimed, "Awesome! A footprint." She snapped a picture of it with her phone. "Looks an awful lot like Eli's footprint, doesn't it?" she asked Sarah.

Sarah surveyed it and nodded. "About his size, and he does wear boots like that."

"It's fresh, too. From last night," Jenna ascertained by touching the soft dirt with her fingertip. "Okay, so we know he made it up here." She stood back up and cast her gaze around for other clues.

"You still smell him, right, girl?" Sarah asked Addie, who was eagerly sniffing the area.

"*I do, really strong,*" Addie agreed.

"What does that mean, really strong? Like he's here in person?" Sarah asked with alarm.

"No." Addie seemed perplexed. "*Just that he stood here for some time.*"

Sarah picked up more leaves and thought she found the edge of another footprint. The mud and the leaves had prevented the footprint from forming clearly, so Sarah could not tell if it was made by the same boot or not. Jenna took a photo of it anyway.

After canvassing the area for some time and finding no evidence of a struggle or foul play, the two women started to head down the other side of the mountain, still searching endlessly. Sarah was developing a headache from focusing her eyes so hard. Addie kept finding a scent trail, then losing it.

"I wonder if this is an older scent trail you're picking up on," Sarah suddenly realized. "That's why you keep losing the scent."

Addie looked up at her dolefully. Then she whined and wagged her tail in fear. She fully shared Sarah's terror of losing Eli.

When they neared the bottom of the mountain, Sarah sat on a fallen log and let out a frustrated sob. "We have just wasted almost three hours! It seems he never came down from the top of the mountain, but where could he have gone, except into that portal?" The last question struck both Sarah and Jenna cold, as they had no idea what that could mean for Eli, or for Witchland as a whole.

"You would have taken less than an hour to find Eli if you had worked with us!" Krell cried.

Sarah started and looked up into the tree. All eight crows were there, looking at her expectantly. "Oh, good, you're here. Can you please help?" Sarah groaned. "We've wasted too much time already, and we know he's in the portal, or on the other side of it, or something . . . We don't know anything," she finally admitted as Krell continued to stare down at her. "We really need help now."

"*First, you must apologize, and then you must do this our way,*" Krell responded.

Sarah let out a strangled groan. "Fine," she said. "If you can help me find him on the other side of the portal, then we will do it your way."

"Uh, so, the crows are talking to you again? Are they going to help at least?" Jenna asked. She knew about Sarah's powers and her ability to speak with animals, though she did not share that ability herself. As the gatekeeper of Witchland, she knew only a few spells that she was tasked with reciting every day to keep Madras out and the town protected from evil. Part of the horrified look on her face, Sarah realized, was because she now wondered if she was to blame for Eli somehow disappearing around the portal.

"They said they will if we do it their way," Sarah replied. "And I have a feeling they are trying to get something in return—image control, if you want to call it that."

Jenna groaned. "Okay, what on earth does that have to do with Eli? We really need to find him."

Sarah sighed. "I know. Let me see if the crows can help."

"Their way had better be worth it," Jenna grunted.

Sarah turned to Krell. "Okay, so how do we do it your way?"

"*First,*" Krell began, "*we're going to ask you a series of questions to educate you about crows. You can educate your friend, Jenna, and Addie, too. Then we want you to promise to take what you learn about us and teach others.*"

"Sure." Sarah nodded. "That seems simple enough." Now she felt guilty for not following along with Krell in the first place. "But what can you do for me in exchange? As in, how will you help Eli?" she added.

"*We know how to open the portal and let you retrieve him,*" Krell replied.

"So he is at the other end of the portal? It won't be too hard to find him?" Sarah asked.

Krell looked at her for a moment, then scooted back on the branch to confer with the other crows. As Sarah, Jenna, and Addie watched impatiently, the crows bobbed up and down, chattering away. Finally, Krell scooted back to the end of his branch and peered down at Sarah. "*We can't tell you that.*"

"You can't or you won't?" Sarah demanded.

"*We can't.*" Krell shrugged his wings, and the other crows raised their voices in agreement. "*We don't know the answer to that. But we can open that portal, the one we saw him get sucked into last night.*"

Sarah translated what he said to Jenna. Jenna's eyes widened with horror, and then she bowed her head, absorbing the sense of guilt clearly overtaking her. "Well, whatever you must do to save him. I'll be your backup. I'm just seriously worried about what might come back through the portal if it is open . . . or what you'll find on the other side."

Sarah felt a deep coldness of fear begin to spread through her body. Her skin started to feel itchy, and she realized that she was starting to turn to wood, a Spellwood response to terror. *Calm,* she told herself as Addie licked her. The wooden sensation began to ease.

"Okay." Sarah turned back to Krell. "We're ready. Ask us the first question."

Sarah and Addie desperately strained to hear what the crows were fervently discussing while Jenna looked on, unable to understand what their caws meant. Previously the birds were loud and disruptive, yet now they kept their cawing low and deliberate. Rather ceremoniously, Krell alighted on Sarah's shoulder and brushed her cheek with his satiny black wing. Sarah realized that she had never been touched by a crow before, and she delighted in how smooth and soft his feathers felt.

"*Firstly, we're not fools. We require a verbal contract to get started. Sarah, as an attorney, do you agree?*"

Sarah nodded impatiently. *What are they going to do, take me to crow court?* she thought sarcastically, but she didn't say it out loud.

"*Sarah and Addie, we crows of the Light Magic Coven have decided to help you find Eli if you agree to change the way in which humans treat and view us. Do you agree?*"

Sarah and Addie both agreed. When Sarah translated for Jenna, she agreed, too.

"*Are you ready to listen?*" Krell then said, boring into Sarah's eyes with his own sharp, intelligent, beady ones.

"No, first, you must tell us what we get in exchange for answering your questions. That's how a proper contract works," Michael spoke up. Sarah started, shocked to hear her deceased mentor's voice, then saw that he had appeared beside her. Michael often came to visit her and help her with her cases as well as protecting Witchland.

Krell pulled in his wing, ruffled his feathers, regained his balance on Sarah's shoulder, and rattled on, "*Good. We have come up with eight questions that you must think about and answer, one by one. You both must agree and solve the questions before you move to the next. If you answer all eight questions correctly, we will share with you a secret spell no human has ever been allowed to use before, a spell that allows you to enter the portal without letting anything get out to this side.*"

"Okay, great, we can all agree with these terms.

Please just start with the questions." Sarah sighed. She felt like screaming with impatience. "We really need that spell to crack open the portal."

Sarah trembled as she recalled her ancestor and Lativia's sister, Madras. Madras was the female version of Voldemort, the evil side to Lativia's goodness. Though Madras practiced dark magic and sorcery, she was a powerful witch and a nearly fair match for Sarah's powers. Defeating her had not been easy; Sarah had prayed and hoped she would never be tested in such a way again. She hated doing battle, especially against her own ancestor, but she also knew that it was her sacred duty to do what she had to do to protect Witchland and its forest. Deep in her gut, even in her bones, she sensed that Madras's dark magic lingered behind all of this. As she tried to puzzle out why, she realized with mounting horror that Madras had either pulled Eli into the portal to hurt Sarah or to bait her to enter the portal. Even more horrifying was the fact that Madras was banished behind the portal, yet somehow able to reach through it to do her foul work.

"*Can you at least tell us what happened to Eli before we begin these questions?*" pleaded Addie.

"*Yes, of course,*" Krell murmured. "*We were actually watching Eli when he was sucked into the portal last night. We tried to stop the abduction, but we didn't have enough power on our own to overcome the para-*

normal binding that got through. We flew to Lativia, and she sent us to you, saying that ghosts can't go through the portal, and you are the one taking care of the town now."

"Did you see who took him?" Sarah asked excitedly.

"Something dark and evil and strong," Krell replied.

"Madras?" Sarah demanded.

"Maybe one of the demons that has become part of her," he agreed.

"It stank," chimed another crow.

"I didn't think birds could smell," Sarah muttered.

Krell puffed up, looking offended. *"We are hardly birds. We are crows. Of course we can smell. We can smell food, fear, and danger. That thing last night smelled like danger."*

"We can smell each other, too," a different crow piped up helpfully. *"We each have our own distinct body odor."*

"It's true," Addie agreed, nodding.

"That's fascinating," Sarah said. "I'm learning so much, but I really want to get to Eli. So let's get on with the questions?"

Just then, Sarah's phone rang. It was her good friend, Daisy. Sarah eagerly answered, hoping Daisy could help. As a fellow member of the Wolf Coven that Lativia had founded, but also hailing from a Haitian voodoo background, Daisy was a powerful witch with an abundant knowledge of herbs that she used in the apothecary she owned.

"Hi, honey. Did you want to grab something at Javacadabra before I open?" Daisy's warm voice flowed through the phone.

"I can't." Sarah rapidly explained what had happened.

"Oh, my stars," Daisy gasped. "We have to go save him."

"I'm trying to find out how from these crows," Sarah responded. "They have a spell to send me through the portal to save him."

"The crows? They're just going to play games with your head! We have to act now!" Daisy cried. "Crows are extremely smart, but they're also known marauders and mischief makers."

All of the crows in the tree began to cry in rage at Daisy's words.

Sarah cringed. "Listen. I'm just as panicked as you are! But I have no idea how to reach into that portal and get him out without Madras making her way back through. Lativia never mentioned anything like this in her spellbook, so unless you know a spell, I need to know what the crows have to teach me."

Daisy sighed long and hard. "I wish I knew a spell, but the only ones I know either banish someone on the other side of a sealed portal, or open the portal back up completely. Obviously we don't want that, but . . . Be very cautious with this, Sarah. I cannot warn you enough. Animal spells don't always translate well to human spells."

"What do you mean?" Sarah felt sick as she looked up at the crows, wondering if they could be trusted. Normally, she trusted animals and knew that they always had the best interest of Witchland at heart, which always aligned with her own interests.

"I don't know what spell they're using on you, so I can't say for certain. I can say that there is a chance you will never get back out of that portal, depending on where it goes and what the crows include in their spell," Daisy explained.

"*Shall we begin?*" Krell said with some indignation. "*Any other interruptions?*"

"Yes," Sarah said. "Please." Then she told Daisy, "I'm sorry, but I have already wasted too much time. Jenna is here to seal the portal after me and to help protect me. I love you, Daisy."

"I love you," Daisy said, her voice caught in a worried sob, as Sarah hung up.

"*I, Krell, as the head of the coven, introduce you to Crow Number One.*" Krell stepped aside and gestured toward another crow, who leaped onto the ground.

"*Greetings, Sarah and Addie,*" the crow squawked. "*Your first question is simply this:*

Upon first glance, we are a bird.
But deep within, there is much berth.
Around us rumors swirl,
But we are as innocent as a squirrel.
We do not bring death,
Bad luck does not flow with our breath.
So what is it that we do? "

"Addie, quick! Do you know the answer?" Sarah lamented that she knew so little about crows.

"*Crows are harbingers,*" Addie said.

"I suppose I knew that," Sarah said guiltily. "I read it in a paranormal law book. But I didn't think much of it."

"*Humans are constantly underestimating us or overestimating us,*" Krell said sadly. "*They think we are evil or that we are pests, but we are sacred portenders of death, danger, and doom. When people see us, though, they think we are the ones causing the death and the danger and the doom! We have our own special abilities, including the ability to predict death, to see and speak with spirits, and to bring news from the other side. Carrion crows often learn from the dead they eat and pass those messages on, as well.*"

"They often come visit me and see what I'm doing," Michael agreed.

"Well, that's good to know." Sarah nodded. "It's a matter of 'don't shoot the messenger!'"

"*Yes, we hate being shot! Now, let's move on to Crow Number Two,*" said Krell.

As if on cue, Crow Number One alighted back on the tree and another crow took her place on the ground. She gazed into Sarah's eyes as she gently whispered:

"Black is not evil. Black is beneficial.
When the light shines bright, what beauty comes from
within?"

At that moment, a shaft of early morning sunlight broke over the trees and struck the back of Crow Number Two. Sarah noticed the gorgeous multicolored sheen reflecting off the crow's back.

"A rainbow!" shouted Sarah, smiling from ear to ear. "Rainbows are symbols of connection; they build bridges between the worlds of humans and animals."

"*Very good,*" Krell said. "*You are a sharp and clever observer of the light. Lativia and your mentor, Michael, told me you were smart; I suppose they may have been right. Now, on to Crow Number Three.*"

"Wait, you even told the crows about me?" Sarah

asked Michael, flattered. Michael had told everyone about her before her arrival in Witchland.

He smiled and nodded gently. Looking at his ghost, Sarah realized how dearly she missed him, with his unkempt hippie hair, half-moon glasses perched on his thin nose, and kind smile. Michael had played a large part in shaping who she was, both as an attorney and as a witch. He was the one who had guided her to finding herself once again. And it was his law firm that she had inherited, which had brought her to Witchland.

"Yes, Michael has always been an advocate for crows, even now that he is a ghost," shared Krell. *"When he was still alive, he worked to save our kind from being shot and poisoned. Our habitats have been preserved in this area because of the work Michael has done for the environment. And we understand you are his protégé, continuing his work after his death. What saddens me is that you don't leave sunflower seeds out for us as Michael once did."* Krell surveyed her sternly over his beak.

"I—I didn't even know Michael did that." Sarah felt worried that the crows must hate her.

"I told you to do that," Michael said sternly.

Sarah felt ashamed. "I'm so sorry. I didn't even hear you. You know I have a lot on my mind all of the time. But you also know that I love animals, and I always set out food for the birds."

"But not the sunflower seeds we like," Krell complained.

"I can certainly start setting out the seeds," Sarah promised.

Jenna sighed with irritation. "Okay, are you guys seriously chatting about bird food right now? Move it along, crows! My partner's life is in danger!"

"What do you think we're asking for when we caw in the woods behind your house?" Crow Number One asked haughtily.

"I'm sorry." Sarah hung her head while making a mental note to buy some dried corn after this whole mess.

"That's better. Now let's not get sidetracked—back to the questions." Krell glanced around with annoyance at not seeing the third crow at his side. *"Crow Number Three, where are you? We are waiting,"* cawed Krell loudly.

"I'm over here in the sun, admiring my rainbow reflection in the porch window," the third crow cawed back. She was the crow who had been pecking at the window. Now, she perched on the end of a branch, where she got the full morning sunshine breaking through the trees from over the peak of Mount Katribus.

"Get over here," Krell said, rolling his eyes and sigh-

ing. *"Sarah and Addie need to hear their third question, and you are up."*

Flying down, Crow Number Three clicked loudly:

"We fly by day rather than night,
To roost in the place where we can listen just

________."

Addie barked loudly, *"I know this one. The answer is right."*

"Oh, yes, yes, that is why you roost in a particular place at night," continued Sarah. "You can listen to what is going on. And last night you chose to roost near the portal so you could help Eli."

Crow Number Four was already perched on one of the tree's large gnarled roots, listening in on the conversation while watching Crow Number Three vainly play with the rainbows reflecting off her feathers. With a slow and steady coo, the fourth crow recited:

"As the sun retreats, our flock flies deep within the trees.
Why do we roost at night so close together?"

"I know you fly by day rather than night so you can hear what the night sounds bring. But maybe you do this to stay warm, and there is safety in numbers?" Sarah said dubiously.

"*Think again, Sarah,*" Krell said. "*Yes, we do stay together for comfort and safety, but there is more to this answer. It pertains to our crime at hand. Think hard about why staying in groups at night is important to us.*"

"I would say you come together at night to talk about what you hear," Sarah said, hoping she got the answer right.

"*And to figure out a plan of action,*" Addie added with her chest puffed out and tail held high with pride.

"*Excellent—the both of you are proving to be capable of changing the way the world views crows. Your answers are thoughtful, and as budding friends of the Light Magic Coven, it is becoming clear you will continue the good work Michael did for us. But we must move on because, as you said before, time is of the essence.*" Krell turned to beckon down the fifth crow.

"*We are ready, Krell. Please give us our next question,*" Addie requested.

"*Crow Number Five is our communication expert. She will share the next question with you,*" Krell announced, nodding respectfully toward the crow who hopped onto the railing next to him.

Crow Number Five preened as she declared:

"*At times of peace, our voices are still.
Yet, when danger lurks, our voices are shrill. Why?*"

"To warn of danger," Sarah said. It seemed like a relatively easy question.

"*Well.*" Addie cocked her head to the right in concentration. "*As a member of the Wolf Coven, I raise the alarm by howling to let my family members know something is happening. When we wolves are silent, we communicate telepathically. And that is when the real business gets done in our coven. I suspect this is true for crows as well.*"

"*Absolutely,*" said Krell. "*Sarah, do you have anything else to add?*"

"No," Sarah said, "but I'm learning so much. Thanks, Krell. I can definitely advocate for you guys better now." She found herself tapping her foot.

"Yes," Michael spoke up, matching Addie's conviction. "Crows have the innate intelligence and skill to recognize when humans or paranormal creatures are threats to the animal kingdom. Most don't know the meaning of nonhuman sounds; therefore, they ignore them. As humans, if we respect our animal friends and learn how we can work as a team in times of peace and danger, we could learn a lot. Both our world and the animal world would be enriched by this newfound cooperation."

"*But instead, people just think we're annoying and a nuisance,*" Krell added.

With their wings flapping and their cawing

increasing in agitation, Sarah wondered if perhaps Michael had said something wrong. The eight birds released their grips on the railing and the branches and ascended in flight while cawing, *"Follow us quickly. Follow us!"*

Sarah, Addie, and Jenna jumped up, racing after Krell and the coven. Michael flowed along behind them on the ethereal wind ghosts used to move about. Sarah knew she must look crazy, dashing down the trail in her slippers and pajamas and coat, alongside a police deputy and a panting dog, and after a flock of noisy and determined crows. At least everyone else in Witchland was eccentric, and they all accepted her funny habits. The only people who might look twice were the tourists who often visited the town to explore its gorgeous scenery and its famous past—including the dwelling place of Lativia Spellwood, the only witch to escape unscathed from the Salem Witch Trials. Such sights were behind the saying, "Weird things happen in Witchland."

Deeper into the forest they loped, with the crows encouraging them to follow. Krell informed them, *"We are now going to the portal. This is where you will discover the answers to your final three questions."*

Running through the woods, Sarah thought of everything she and Addie had done for this town. She loved it here, and she was downright determined to save Eli from the unknown ghost that had illegally slipped through the portal. With wolf-like speed and agility, she leaped over the rocks and fallen trees in her way. As a shapeshifter, she was able to channel her Spellwood Wolf Coven powers even though she remained in her human form.

"Attagirl, Sarah. You understand how wolves and crows work together! Even though you need to solve three more questions, you are getting close," rattled the crows in approval.

As a new crow took the lead, Sarah asked Krell, "What is happening, Krell? The crows seem anxious."

"We have to get to the portal immediately," Krell cawed with intensity. *"Crow Number Six is leading the way. Follow him, as he is the head sentry. His job is to forewarn the coven of danger. We must not delay."*

"Why? Has something else happened?" Sarah cried.

"What happened?" Jenna yelled.

"We can sense he is in pain," Krell answered.

Sarah cried out. "Crow Number Six, while we are following you, please tell Addie and me the next question. We can't afford to waste time," Sarah yelled.

Without looking back from his flight path, Crow Number Six cawed:

"Portal of danger, we do protect.
To ease the path between life and death.
We do not soften blows;
We simply warn with our crows.
Why?"

Out of breath, Sarah whispered to Addie, "Since Crow Number Six is the head sentry and warns the others of danger, and crows have been unfairly judged for centuries to be evil as well as a sign that someone is going to die, do you think they're just bringing us here to witness Eli's death?"

"No, Sarah, trust the crows. They are on our side. Remember, they were sent by Lativia," Addie warned sagely.

"Krell, I have the answer!" Sarah said. "As you said earlier, crows have a special ability to learn about evil in advance and protect us from it. Crows are not the cause of evil; they are the harbingers of evil's advance. Their intent is always to protect us. They guard portals between life and death in order to keep the balance of things, but they don't cause death."

"Sarah, you are correct, but look ahead to see where your crow family has landed," Krell said. *"Crow Number Seven is eagerly waiting to share your next question."*

"*Greetings, Sarah and Addie,*" Crow Number Seven cooed. "*We have reached the portal.*"

Sarah anxiously crouched before the two stones marking the portal's entrance. Addie whined fearfully while Jenna wrung her hands. Michael hung back, watching the whole thing with a tense expression on his face.

"*Crow Number Seven, please reveal the question to Sarah and Addie—without delay,*" Krell cawed with determination.

"In a murder we fly.
But sometimes we are alone.
Why?"

"Teamwork is always better," Sarah said, now panting slightly as she leaned against the rough rocks. Running up the mountain was always a challenge, though she had done it more times than she could count. "But when you're alone, you can get more food without competition?"

"*You are absolutely right, Sarah. So why do you always insist on doing things with your coven when you don't need to, and then doing things on your own when you need help?*"

Sarah paused before glancing at Michael and Jenna guiltily. She did have a tendency to do things on her own, more out of a sense of urgency than any sort of misguided sense of independence. "Can I use their help now, in the portal?" she asked.

"*Of course. Jenna can guard it, ensuring nothing gets out. Michael cannot cross through the portal; portals tend to suck in ghosts and never let them go, and they may even destroy the spirit, for ghosts are weaker than humans. Addie may go with you to offer you protection. But you seem to be forgetting someone,*" Krell hinted.

"Of course I haven't forgotten you eight crows," Sarah said. "You guys have helped me immensely. I couldn't have gotten here without you. So, do you want to join me in the portal?"

"*Of course not,*" all of the crows unanimously agreed. "*But we appreciate the invitation,*" Crow Number Four added. "*We don't get invited to much, so that means a lot.*"

"*Now you have answered the first seven questions correctly,*" Krell cawed. "*You understand who we are and our importance in the world—and how we improve it for the greater good. Now let us show you how we can help you save Eli.*"

"Thank you, Krell. We are ready. We definitely believe in the magic and wisdom of crows. Addie and I are of service to make the world a better place for all crows. We are tired of the misconception humans have that you are evil and malicious," Sarah said ceremoniously, with Addie barking in agreement.

"Please prepare yourselves for your final question," Krell cawed. *"The answer to this question unlocks the secret spell of the Light Magic Coven. Once spoken by you with a clear and powerful intention, it will open this portal."*

Sarah thought of Daisy's warning and felt her stomach tighten. Her skin began to harden, and it took extra effort this time to not turn to wood. *What if this animal magic backfires?* she thought with panic.

Krell was breathtakingly beautiful as he landed on Sarah's shoulder. With Addie leaning on Sarah's leg, the three of them looked deep into each other's eyes. It was then that the recognition of their heart-bonded kinship was made. Sarah knew she found family, and nothing was going to stop her from saving Eli.

"You are my new animal spirit guide," Sarah realized, recognizing the bond as the same one she shared with the wolves and lynx.

Flapping his majestic wings, Krell recited the final question with a deep and melodious boom that brought all the other crows into a circle around the portal. Jenna looked on, her mouth hanging open and her hands trembling.

"What do crows hold in their feathers to dispel the darkness caused by the shadow of evil?"

"Well, the rainbows . . ." Sarah began.

"Plus, we know how crows listen to each other and work together to vanquish evil and warn humans in order to protect them," Addie added.

"We have the answer!" Sarah declared. "Because crows' feathers are black, they absorb all light. And since crows have their own magical powers, they can use the light to do good in the world when needed. So you have magic locked in your feathers."

Krell's plumage shone with rainbows as he plucked one of his tail feathers with his beak and offered it to Sarah. *"Let this be your guiding light in the portal,"* he told her.

"Wait, so the other side is dark?" Sarah said with dismay. "Where does it lead?"

"I can't tell you that; no one knows," Krell replied. *"It is an underworld where crows don't go."*

"An underworld?" Sarah cried. "As in, Hell, the bad place?"

"Something like it," Crow Number Four spoke up.

Krell simply waved his wing to dismiss Sarah's fears. *"You have to be brave and go in and find Eli."*

"But Madras might be somewhere on the other side, and I don't have my coven or Lativia's spellbook to help me," Sarah said, a slight tremble audible in her voice. Jenna placed a reassuring hand on her shoulder but didn't say anything.

"*Are you scared?*" one of the other crows taunted.

"Of course," Sarah replied. She swallowed. "But I am also brave, and I will do this, for Eli." She began to dredge up all of her courage and recite various spells in her mind that she had learned, anything that might prove useful in a fight against Madras.

"*Very good. You have proved yourself to us, and you have our aid,*" Krell told her. "*You can rely on your newfound crow knowledge and your instincts to guide and protect you.*"

He then told her to repeat after him:

"Corvidi es veritas
Plumae semper niger
Sed ditavi Abram lux coacervabitur tibi
Tenere la potentia a liberati omnis
Di hominis incarcerate."

CHAPTER FOUR

As Krell's voice resounded with the last croaked word, the air above the stones became to shimmer, much like a heat mirage. Sarah and Addie stared in fascination as the shimmery air began to ripple and swirl, like a strange phantasma or a melting mirror.

One of the ripples in the center began to blacken and widen. Sarah stared at it with mounting horror. With a sharp tearing sound, the tear began to open into a large hole, much like paper being torn. Suddenly, Sarah felt a sucking sensation pulling her toward the hole.

Sarah screamed in shock as the force of the hole began to suck her skin, pulling out her lips and cheeks in an uncomfortable pucker. Addie yelped as the force also pulled her fur toward the tunnel. Without warning, the force became extremely strong and ripped them both off of their feet. With a gut-wrenching sensation, Sarah felt the air rush past her and change as she entered a new atmosphere.

They tumbled headfirst into the portal. Sarah realized that she might lose Krell's feather, so she clutched it to her body so hard that it made her hand hurt.

With a squelching sound like mud around a shoe, the light of the world behind them blinked out. The portal door had already sucked shut behind them, and Sarah suddenly wondered how she could have forgotten to ask the crows how to get back out of this portal. The sucking force ceased, and Sarah and Addie dropped to the ground. A pointy rock bruised Sarah's hip. "Ouch!" she cried, rolling on her side and rubbing the bruise. Then she realized that she and Addie were encapsulated in total darkness. Panic gripped her heart.

"*It's dark,*" Addie whined fearfully.

Sarah held up the feather, and rainbow light erupted from its blackness. It illuminated what appeared to be a dark earthen tunnel or cave, with tree branches and rocks making up the supporting arches of the roof. It smelled dank, like a fetid marsh that had been hidden from the sun for a long time. Clammy air stuck to Sarah's skin, weighing down her frizzy red curls. At the edge of the circle of illumination, there was only pitch blackness.

"Eli?" Sarah called.

Her voice echoed, only hinting at the depth of the tunnel.

Trembling, she clambered up onto her feet and tried to brush some of the mud stuck to her pants off. Addie hugged her side closely as she cautiously made her way forward. The mud squished and splashed under Sarah's and Addie's steps. The dank smell only became stronger, coating their faces like masks of reek. Sarah held the inside of her elbow over her nose to keep out the stench. "Addie, how can you stand this?" she cried.

"Things aren't stinky to me the same way they are to you," Addie replied. *"I smell the many layers of scent, and the information each layer contains."*

Sarah sighed. "I wish I had that ability, but I don't. It's just one big blanket layer of stinky to me."

"I can smell water and frogs and salamanders," Addie went on excitedly.

"Interesting. So this place seems like a real cave. I was honestly expecting something like fire and brimstone, to be honest." She glanced around at the dirt, stone, and root walls. The tunnel appeared to be almost perfectly round and descending. There was a clear sensation of being deep underground. Sarah wondered how deep they really were, and how far down the tunnel traversed. Would the air even be breathable at the bottom?

"*Smells like it,*" Addie answered.

"How about Eli? Can you smell him?" Sarah was frustrated that the feather only illuminated a circle of a few feet around her. She stepped carefully, trying not to slip or lose a shoe in the mire underfoot. The awareness that Madras, or any other kind of entity or dangerous animal, might be lurking in the shadows made treading forward difficult. Sarah kept fighting the urge to turn to wood, or at least turn back and run for her life. *I'm trapped down here, and I don't know how to get out,* she kept thinking. *The way out is sealed shut behind us to keep Madras out, but that means we're kept out, too! How did I not think of this before agreeing to this?*

"No," Addie said sadly. "*Sorry, I forgot for a second what we were doing. I got too caught up in the excitement of all the smells.*"

Sarah rolled her eyes. "Makes sense. Now, this is the portal where they banished Madras. I didn't know they sent her to some underground cave. We have to watch out for her *and* find Eli. Is this just one long tunnel, you think?"

"*I think it opens up into a cave with a river. I can hear running water and echoes,*" Addie replied.

Sure enough, Sarah was soon able to hear what

Addie was referring to. She felt the narrow walls of the tunnel widen on either side of her, and she suddenly slipped on mud that was even slicker than the mud of the tunnel. Addie slipped behind her. They skidded down a mudbank and plopped into a pool of shallow, cool water.

Something brushed Sarah's face, and she screamed. When she whacked at it out of instinct, her fingers became covered in green slime. "Algae," she muttered to Addie, who had started paddling through the water beside her. "At least I know the underworld is somewhat like the, uh, I guess you call it the above world? Same plants and whatnot, at least."

"*Maybe we should call above the sunlight world,*" Addie replied. "*And this is the world that doesn't exist in the sun, where things go to hide.*"

Sarah shuddered. "That is a disturbing thought." She held up the feather again and saw that the pool they were in was covered in a thick layer of multicolored algae. Swimming through it was uncomfortable, and Sarah worried about what may lurk hidden underneath the slime. Visions of prehistoric fish with razor-sharp teeth flitted through her mind.

She rapidly cut through the fetid, slime-covered water and clambered onto the opposite bank. She and Addie slipped many times before finally locating their footing on the slippery rocks. She held the feather over-head and illuminated the cave chamber they were in.

It was a vast chamber with black mold and slime coating the walls. A stand of strange black trees grew toward the ceiling in the center of the chamber and some other black plant-like beings snaked across the ground, like vines. Water dripped down from the ceiling, forming stalactites and stalagmites. They were not very big, suggesting the cave was not too old geologically.

When she illuminated the ceiling, she realized it was covered in black forms hanging upside down. Bats! She realized the stink within the cave was not only the standing water and slime, but also guano. She was thankful that Krell's feather was dim enough to not disturb the bats from their daytime slumber.

"So if there are bats, then there must be some exit point." Sarah breathed out a sigh of relief.

"*I can't smell fresh air, but I'm sure there is,*" Addie agreed. "*This chamber doesn't seem as dark as the tunnel.*"

"It is a bit lighter, isn't it?" Sarah smiled, feeling overcome with joy knowing that finding her way out of here was at least possible.

But then another troubling thought occurred to her: She did not know where this underground place was, and how far it was from Witchland. What if she emerged with Eli and Addie, and they found themselves in a foreign country where she didn't understand the language? Finding her way back home would not be particularly easy, especially since she did not have a credit card or passport on her person, and she was pretty sure Eli didn't, either. Explaining how they had gotten there to customs would most definitely not be fun. Hopefully her phone would work, now that it had been submerged in water. Though it was supposed to be waterproof, Sarah did not trust such claims on electronics.

"Why did I agree to this?" Sarah groaned to Addie.

"To rescue Eli," Addie responded happily. None of these worries concerned her; she was content just knowing that the above world was accessible from this cave.

"Yes, of course, but there had to have been another way to rescue Eli." Sarah shook her head. "I suppose we need to search this chamber?"

"Let's do it."

Sarah began to walk into the center of the cavern. Moss and vines felt slippery under her feet, and the way was treacherous. To her left, a river of dark but clean-looking water gushed past, headed toward a black hole in the cave wall. The river did not feed any of the smelly, fetid pools dotting the chamber's floor. By the distant roaring sound, Sarah could tell the river cascaded into a waterfall somewhere beyond the hole, though it sounded fairly far away.

Sarah stopped at the edge of the trees, unwilling to enter their foreboding darkness. From this vantage point, she could not see the walls of the chamber well enough to make any judgments about how to make her way out of here. After calling to Eli a few times with no answer, she and Addie cautiously made their way to the edge of the chamber and began to slowly circle it. Their path was soon disrupted by the river, which seemed deep, fast, and not crossable, but Sarah had already seen two small cave tunnels leaving the chamber, as well as the impassable cave that the river disappeared into. Being underground had disoriented her sense of direction so much that she could no longer tell which of the two caves she had spotted was the one she and Addie had entered through. Either way, that tunnel would not be possible to climb with its slick mud going uphill, and it was sealed off, so it was not much use to them.

"I don't see Eli anywhere," Sarah said. "Maybe he's in that stand of trees?"

"*I don't smell him,*" Addie agreed worriedly.

"I just hope he's in here and we don't have to climb through one of those caves. I don't trust unknown caves. There can be poisonous gases or snakes or sharp drops . . ." Sarah began to creep toward the center again, this time determined to enter the dark woods that stood there.

Her blood ran cold when she distinctly heard a witch's cackle.

"Addie! Hide! It might be Madras!" Sarah shouted.

But Addie was already running into the patch of trees. To Sarah's horror, she disappeared among their scaly trunks into the gloom.

With no choice but to run after her dog, Sarah gave chase. Her feet repeatedly got stuck in vines or sank into the mud. Her socks and running shoes were positively caked in filth when she finally reached the clearing where Addie stood, sniffing something—or someone.

Her hand trembled as she raised the feather and peered through the shadows. Her heart raced. What would she do if she came face to face with Madras, her great nemesis? She felt horribly unprepared, without even Lativia's spellbook to aid her.

A dim green light illuminated a clearing in the center of the trees. Sarah cautiously stepped closer and realized the light was emanating from a crystal hanging from a hooked pole. Next to the pole was a bent figure with . . . a slouchy black witch hat and a crow on her shoulder. The figure was petting Addie, who was wagging her tail and licking her hand.

"Harriet?" Sarah gasped out loud at the sight of the

tiny Witchland witch, who always seemed to show up at inconvenient times and have something to say about Sarah's attire.

Harriet let out another cackle, which echoed eerily off the cave walls, as she straightened her back. Her back always had a slight stoop in it, however, making her appear even shorter than she really was. Sarah practically towered over her at five-foot-six. "You two be quiet! You're scaring off Edgar's glowworms," Harriet snapped.

The crow on Harriet's shoulder, Edgar, bobbed up and down. *"That's Krell's feather. Krell's feather, that is,"* he told Harriet.

"What on earth are you doing here?" Sarah demanded.

"Yeah, are you looking for Eli, too?" Addie asked, sitting down.

"Of course not, why would I be?" Harriet said. "I'm hunting glowworms. They're Edgar's favorite thing to eat."

"So . . . I thought this was the underworld? What are you doing here, then?" Sarah could not believe that another citizen of Witchland, the rather annoying and smart-alecky witch Harriet, was comfortably frequenting this disturbing place. *How does she know about it, and how did she get here?* she thought.

Harriet looked at her strangely, then began to

guffaw. She slapped her knee. Edgar bounced up and down on her shoulder, laughing along. "An underworld? You city slickers sure are hilarious. You act like this is the gateway to Hades's underworld or Dante's Seven Circles of Hell or something!"

Sarah did appreciate how well read Harriet was. "Well, it seems like it. The crows said it was an underworld."

"*They don't know what they're talking about. Scaredy birds,*" Edgar croaked with laughter.

"What is this place, if it's not the underworld?" Sarah ventured.

"It's a cave under Mount Katribus." Harriet shook her head, chuckling. "City slickers. Why didn't you bring your heels down here?"

Sarah rolled her eyes. Her professional and groomed appearance had been very important to her when she had lived in New York, and Harriet had given her much grief for her expensive Jimmy Choo heels when Sarah had first moved to Witchland. In fact, Harriet gave her grief for everything.

"So this is just a cave? I thought it was an underworld place where evil lives," Sarah said, bewildered. "The crows led me here to find Eli; he disappeared through Madras's portal. I went through it, and now I'm here."

"*Krell,*" cawed Edgar.

"Krell must've shown you a shortcut. I climbed down the long way." Harriet raised her lamp and muttered a spell that made it brighten considerably. From its increased light, Sarah could see several other tunnels led into the chamber. One looked slightly less dim than the others, and Harriet indicated that one. "That way leads back to town. Comes out of a crevice in a rock behind a fallen tree near my hut. It's the way out, unless you want to stay here and become a glowworm."

"Do you know where the other tunnels go?" Sarah peered around at the five other ones, wondering which one she had emerged from.

"All around under the mountain and beyond. It's a big cave system. The best nematodes can be found down that one. Edgar likes nematodes as well." Harriet pointed at one of the other tunnels.

"*Nematodes,*" Edgar said hungrily. "*Tell Krell he's missing out on the nematodes,*" he added as an aside to Sarah.

"Krell and his wife abandoned my Edgar when he was a baby because he had a broken wing and some brain damage. He was hit by a car while his mother was teaching him to fly. I mended him up; now he's my familiar," Harriet said proudly. She started to make her way toward the tunnel with the best nematodes.

Sarah awkwardly followed before Harriet turned

and asked, "If you're going to come along, then I'll gladly have you pick the nematodes off the rocks for me. They're sticky buggers."

"No worries, I'm good. I'm trying to do something else." Sarah hung back.

"Suit yourself!" Harriet gave a final cackle. The darkness returned as Harriet moved farther and farther away with her light crystal and her basket of glow-worms. Sarah held the feather up again, though her arm was getting tired.

"*What should we do?*" Addie inquired anxiously, standing dutifully at Sarah's side.

"Can you try tracking Eli again?" Sarah begged.

"*I really can't smell him over the frogs and fish and bats and worms down here,*" Addie said apologetically.

Just then, Sarah could hear Eli yelling, "Help! Help! Someone please come help me!" There was the sound of his radio turning off. He was trying to phone for help on his radio, and he couldn't get a signal in the caves.

Sarah and Addie began to lope in the direction of his voice. "I'm coming!" Sarah shouted, feeling braver now that she had met Harriet in the cave. She didn't feel the need to be quiet anymore. If they were under Mount Katribus, then surely Madras couldn't be in here, for the Leekins had banished her from the woods a few months ago. Addie barked along with her, her deep dog voice echoing off of the dripping walls.

The direction they were running toward turned out to be another cave, exiting the big chamber. It was drier and easier to traverse as it sloped uphill. Sarah and Addie ran up it, and it veered left. Sarah realized this tunnel must cross over the tunnel that the river gushed into below. Her shoes made a disgusting slurping sound as she ran, and she groaned when she thought of how much mud she and Addie would track into the house later. "You are going to need a bath, girl!" she told Addie.

But her relief was immediately replaced by horror when suddenly she felt nothing under her feet at all. She was falling through the air but could feel rocks scraping at her skin! She and Addie splashed into deep water in total blackness. Sarah struggled against the current, but it was much too fast for her, and the darkness prevented her from getting her bearings. Somewhere ahead of her, at an uncertain distance, she could hear the waterfall roaring and crashing down what sounded like a significant drop.

"Addie!" she shrieked.

Addie was being rushed along by the current, her eyes wide with terror. Sarah grabbed her and held her shaking body close as the swift current carried them through a very dark tunnel. Sarah had dropped the feather, but she could see it being carried through the water up ahead. She tried to swim to it but got sucked underwater. Desperate to remain on the surface, she swam back up and gripped Addie again. She gritted her teeth and shut her eyes. *Great Goddess, if only I could grab that feather!*

With a violent swoop, the two were caught up in the waterfall. Sarah felt as if the world had been ripped out from under her as she wooshed down. Water got into her eyes and her mouth, and she tried her hardest not to breathe any more in. With a nauseating plummet, both Sarah and Addie plunged into a deep pool.

Sarah looked above her and saw only darkness, but she could feel the bubbles rising around her and Addie. With a fervent upward stroke, she managed to break the surface of the water. Gasping in air, she looked around for Addie, who soon surfaced next to her. Already, though, they were being pulled apart by a rapid whirlpool. Sarah realized that they were in another cave chamber, and she could see better. This cave had a distinct glow, though from what source, Sarah could not yet identify.

Swimming along the circulating current, Sarah managed to reach Addie and grasp her. But when she tried to break free of the current and make for the rocky shore, the whirlpool simply spun her around and around. The spinning was making her horribly dizzy, and she couldn't stop coughing from the water in her lungs.

She remembered something about how to swim through riptides and thought it might help here. "Addie, we're going to have to swim at an angle!" Sarah cried. "We have to cut through the current of the whirlpool."

Addie was too panicked to listen. She kept flailing at the water with her front legs. Sarah was drenched, and the weight of the water in her clothes, as well as Addie's weight, made staying above the water difficult.

"Addie, you have to calm down!" Sarah cried.

Addie continued to struggle.

Sarah shut her eyes and began to recite a spell to relax Addie. As Addie suddenly relaxed, she also became heavier. Sarah gave a cry of desperation and began to cut through the current at a sharp angle, lugging Addie along with her.

Sarah finally managed to get Addie safely on shore. Gasping for breath and soaked, she pushed Addie onto the edge, then clambered up next to her dog. She collapsed in exhaustion next to Addie, her arms and back aching, her body covered in bruises.

The spell wore off Addie, and she leaped up, shaking her fur vigorously. Sarah found herself even more soaked as the water droplets rained over her.

"Addie, stop!" she protested. "I'm already soaked and cold!"

"*Whew! That was close!*" Addie gasped. "*I really thought we were done for.*"

"We are sure lucky there were no sharp rocks or anything at the bottom of the waterfall," Sarah replied. Then she returned to the edge of the pool, looking for the feather. She spotted it rotating in the whirlpool. Using a simple summoning spell, Sarah mentally pulled it out of the water and through the air toward her. She recalled another spell and used it to become dry again.

"*Thank you!*" Addie said after Sarah used the drying spell on her, as well.

"I think we're even farther from Eli than before, and he was crying for help." Sarah began to sob. "What if something bad was happening to him? I'm so frustrated!"

Addie came over and licked Sarah's face. Sarah smiled down at her. "You smell like wet dog even now that you're dry," she commented.

"*Thanks! I love that smell.*" Addie laughed.

Even when she was upset, Addie always managed to find a way to make her smile. "Let's get back to business. We have to figure out how to get out of here and make our way to Eli!"

Just as she said this, she noticed something glinting

behind Addie. Curious, she raised the feather and began to stumble forward, her body still nearly paralyzed with exhaustion and stress. When she got close enough to the glint, she realized it was a mirror on a stand, and its surface seemed to reflect . . . deep green water? Sarah stepped forward and felt the eerie sensation of passing through an invisible barrier, where the air became drastically drier.

"Did you feel that?" she asked Addie.

Addie barked affirmatively and wagged her tail. "*It feels much nicer in here now,*" she commented.

Sarah cautiously touched the mirror, and it rippled under her fingertips. The ripples spread out slowly, reaching the wooden frame of the mirror. Then its surface became reflective, and Sarah saw herself and Addie, but also something else very strange behind her.

She gasped and wheeled around on her heels. Behind her was an arrangement of lavish furniture. There was a chair, upholstered in red velvet, and a four-poster bed with a lavish gold brocade canopy. On a beautiful carved mahogany dining table, sat several unlit candles, and a chandelier dangled from above, suspended from apparently nothing. When Sarah cautiously touched the furniture, she realized that it was dry. The ground was dry, too. She glanced back at the pool from which she and Addie had come and noticed the outline of a clear bubble. They were inside some sort of magical bubble, intended to keep this little bedroom safe from the damp of the cave.

"What is this place?" Sarah asked Addie.

Addie wagged her tail. "*I don't know, but isn't it strange? Who would live down here?*"

Sarah began to scan the furniture carefully, hoping to find some sort of clue as to its underground occupant, though she already knew it belonged to someone with magical powers.

With trepidation, she felt around and under furniture. There was a heavy, dark vibe to the place that reminded her of her demonic ancestor. "I don't like this at all. I think this may be where Madras has been staying," Sarah whispered. "But then how could that be? She's banished."

"*Why are you whispering? If it is Madras's place, she probably already knows we are here,*" Addie told her.

Sarah shuddered. "I really don't feel prepared for this," she whispered. Then she regretted it; if Madras could hear her, then she knew Sarah was afraid, and she would exploit that weakness. Madras was famous for exploiting people's weaknesses. "Hopefully she used to live here and doesn't anymore."

"*The furniture looks awfully clean, and it smells like someone was here recently, though I can't tell who,*" Addie replied. "*Madras's scent shifts a lot*" *depending on which demon is predominant at the time."*

As Sarah thought about that and explored the strange little home, she realized, with horror, that this may have all been an elaborate trap. By stealing Eli, Madras had managed to lure Sarah into her home. That made Sarah easier to defeat. *I'm not afraid. I must remain strong and undefeated!* Sarah thought, instantly steeling herself. She began to mentally list spells she could use against Madras again. "If she is down here, then I have to banish her for good," she promised herself.

Underneath the bed, her hands knocked against a trunk. She pulled it out and opened it to reveal a large collection of dark crystals cut in various shapes. There was also a crystal ball carved of dark red agate. When she held it before her eyes, she saw nothing. *Hmm, I must not be able to use divination powers. At least, not yet. That's definitely something to look into and start learning.*

"Addie, this place definitely belongs to a witch." Sarah nodded. "I think it really is Madras's home."

"Could it belong to Harriet?" Addie suggested.

"I don't know why Harriet would have a place like this when she has a hut in Witchland. Besides, it doesn't feel like her . . . vibe. She does not strike me as the type to be into lavish velvet and brocade silks, you know?"

"*I agree,*" Addie said.

Sarah looked back into the trunk and realized there was one final item at its very bottom: a leather-bound journal. Its cover was encrusted in little jewels. Sarah pulled it out and attempted to open it, but the lock would not budge. She began to feel around in the trunk for a key when Addie pointed out, "*There's no keyhole. It's a magic journal!*"

"I wish I had thought of that in high school when I would write about my secret crush," Sarah joked. She shut her eyes tight and began to think hard about spells that unlocked things. She mumbled a few, but the journal remained shut tight.

"Let's try music!" Sarah did not have her phone working to play songs, so instead she began to sing. Her voice started shaky and high-pitched. Addie cocked her head at Sarah before pointing her nose at the ceiling and howling.

"Why do dogs always howl along to singing?" Sarah asked.

"*Isn't that what you're doing? I'm just singing along,*" Addie replied, seeming confused by the question.

The journal remained locked.

Sarah began to feel a prickle up her spine. "Addie, I

really am starting to get weird vibes from this place. Familiar vibes. Like . . . I think we're being watched."

Addie gulped.

Sarah rose and shined the feather's light on the bed. She realized that the place was very clean, as if someone had been keeping it up. "And someone has been here recently. Possibly even last night." Then she shook her head. "This doesn't make sense. If this cave is under Mount Katribus, and Madras was banished, how is she here?"

"*We drifted a long way on the river,*" Addie reminded her. "*Maybe we're out of Witchland now?*"

"And the Leekins did say that they didn't know where they banished her; she just went somewhere else, out of the woods! The Leekins can't control anywhere else," Sarah mused. "And Madras mentioned she lived in caves when we were battling her. Maybe she's living here, just outside of the boundary of the Mount Katribus woods."

Addie began to whine. "*I don't like this at all.*"

"I don't either. I think we stumbled upon Madras's lair."

CHAPTER FIVE

Sarah carried the journal over to the mirror, which was green again, and touched it once more. It rippled again under her touch, and she felt a cold chill run up her arm. Unable to think of what to say, she was reminded of a Disney movie. "Mirror, mirror, on the wall, who is the fairest of them all?"

The mirror suddenly turned translucent, and then a solid image appeared of Madras herself. The last time Sarah had seen her, she had looked sickly, a ghost torn apart by multiple demons who had laid claim to her existence. Now, in the mirror, she looked healthy and was wearing a green velvet cloak, closed at the throat with a massive gold brooch. Her cheeks were rouged richly, and her red hair was piled on top of her head in a beautiful updo. Sarah cringed away from the mirror, thinking it was really Madras inside, before realizing the image was making the same movements over and over. It was a trapped image of Madras preening herself, checking her face, patting her hair, delighting in the way her cloak swirled around her legs when she twirled side to side.

"I can't wait for the dance. All of the men are going to love me." A dreamy voice floated out of the mirror. Though the voice was so different from the eerie dissonance of Madras's voice during the battle, it was indeed her, admiring how pretty she was. Sarah suppressed another shudder. "They are going to flock to me instead of my drab sister Lativia! She can't steal any more boyfriends from me! I'll be the one doing the stealing." Then the image threw its head back and laughed vainly. "Ah, yes, I'm the most beautiful of them all!"

"I think this mirror shows Madras what she wants to see. It lets her live in her jealous fantasies over and over." Sarah gasped. "How unsettling is that, Addie!?"

Addie woofed in agreement. *"I'm glad you're not like that! Even though you do spend a lot of time in front of the mirror!"*

Madras's copy in the mirror suddenly pulled the journal from under her cloak and said, "Witch hazel." It sprang open. Sarah excitedly held up the journal and said the same words. It unlocked, and its pages fell open to the last entry, where Madras had marked her place with a beautiful leather bookmark.

The entry was dated just a few days before. Sarah read, *They can try to keep me out of Witchland, but I'll just steal away the town's security, one by one. Soon, there will be no one left to defend the town. I almost beat the Leekins this time. I'm not worried about them.*

Sarah groaned. "Oh, hex my lucky stars—it is Madras, plotting to get back into Witchland. That's why she took Eli, because he is one of the town's protectors and, without him, Witchland is weaker."

"She might also have known kidnapping him would make you come down here," Addie said cautiously.

Sarah suddenly got chills. "That's definitely a possibility I have considered."

She flipped through the journal entries, hoping for some other clues. The entries were mostly jealous meanderings, or vainglorious gloating.

Madras had been positively sure she would win the town from her sister and turn its magical citizens to her dark side. The first entry was shortly before she had enchanted Jason Gonforth and Mayor Lewis. It detailed her sickening reasoning and her plot to take over the forest, making it a haven for greed and evil. *I will make this place so much better than my sister ever did. Goodbye to all these la-di-da small businesses and the sawmill and the wishy-washy "Lativian" witches with their silly herbal concoctions. Madras is coming to town, and she will get rich! I just need to find a woman to possess so that I can be there in human form and enjoy all of the luxuries I plan to buy. I will become the owner of all of the businesses and live in a beautiful mansion on top of Mount Katribus, right where my silly sister sits on her contrived throne with her weird little ghost court of has-beens. Guess what, Lativia, you're not the true queen of magic like you claim, because you gave yourself that title and no one has ever challenged you for it! This crown is my birthright because I'm the eldest and the better witch, but unlike you, I have had to fight for it, and I will earn it.*

"I am so glad that she didn't get to do any of this." Sarah shook her head. "I can't believe she wanted to tear down our beautiful forest, just to live in some mansion in the ghosts' clearing and get rich. And I'm glad she didn't get to possess some poor woman and take over her body."

"We need to make sure she can't ever make any of these fantasies come true," Addie growled. *"If she tries, you can be sure I will make her accountable!"*

For the next several entries, Madras gloated about how her plan was working perfectly. She mentioned how she had spied on Sarah, which made Sarah shiver. *I definitely need to buy better blinds and use some sort of enchantment on my mirrors to make sure Madras can't see me,* Sarah thought.

Then Madras had scribbled furiously about how Sarah and Lativia and the others had beaten her in battle on top of the peak. *I loathe my sister more than anything in the world! She will never let me have what is mine! But one day, I will vanquish her! I am sure that little troublemaker Sarah will come over to my side! She wants power as much as I do. I see myself in her. With her and the Leekins behind me, I will rule the world!*

"Ha, not a chance of that ever happening." Sarah snorted. "There is none of me in that woman! Or spirit or whatever she is now." She shook her head but read on. Getting inside Madras's head made her feel sick and disgusted, but it was also enlightening. *Know your enemies,* Sarah thought, wisdom that Michael had drilled into her head in law school. Knowing her enemies is how she often won in court, and now it would help her with her archnemesis.

The entries after Madras's defeat were depressed and full of self-loathing and poisonous rumination. Sarah felt sorry for her ancestor as she flipped through the pages, but she also felt like rolling her eyes. "I can't believe she doesn't see how pathetic her whining is. She could have done so much with her life, but all she chose to do was envy her sister," Sarah commented.

"Envy is the death of many people who could have

been great," Addie agreed glumly. *"It's so sad, the way Madras thinks and feels."*

"Yeah, her ego is terribly fragile." Sarah sighed. "I've never met someone that unhappy in my life. Even though she's just a ghost, she's still got a lot of issues."

After reaching the last entry that she had already read, Sarah slammed the journal closed. "How frustrating. I really wish she had written where she was keeping Eli. I really hope she's not hurting him in any way."

"Sarah, watch out!" Addie cried.

Sarah wheeled around to see a figure with red hair in green velvet land on the ground behind her. Looking straight at Sarah, Madras snarled and then threw her head back, laughing.

Sarah's heart began hammering, and she had to force herself to stay calm and collected. There was no use losing her wits while facing her nemesis. "Madras, where is Eli?"

"All you care about is Eli," Madras seethed. Her voice sounded strange, like a series of snakes hissing.

"You didn't honestly expect to kidnap Eli and not have me come rescue him, did you?" Sarah snorted. "You know I love him very much."

"But you have a whole legacy to live up to! Being distracted by men won't do you any good!" Madras cried.

"Lativia married and had two sons," Sarah answered. "And she's still the most powerful witch of all time."

That was salt in the wound. Madras recoiled, then resumed her haughty taunts. "Why are you going through my things, then, unless you secretly want to be me?"

"What? I'm just trying to get inside your head, find out what you're up to," Sarah said, flabbergasted that Madras could misconstrue her actions so utterly.

"Right," Madras said sarcastically. "You have always been obsessed with me since you first heard of me. Evil is so much more fun and seductive than boring old good, don't you agree?"

"*Not at all*," Addie growled. She had placed herself between Madras and Sarah protectively. Her hackles prickled up.

"I would rather be good than evil any day, no matter how fun and seductive evil might be." Sarah glanced up and down her ancestor, who looked particularly sickly. No wonder her skin was so pale, living down in a cave. "Honestly, you don't seem to be having much fun down here, anyway."

"That's because my vile sister took everything that was rightfully mine," Madras shot back. "But I will reclaim it! And I want my darling sister's descendant to help me."

"That will never happen. Now tell me where Eli is, and I will let you go without a fight," Sarah replied. She had a feeling that she and Madras were about to battle, no matter what. Her goal was to avoid using force and violence as much as possible, and to avoid caving in fear. The one thing she counted on was that Madras was weakened by her recent defeat on Mount Katribus and her lack of support in this secluded cave.

"Oh, you can't just *have* your man back," Madras said, pretending to yawn. "I rather like having such a handsome man down here to keep me company. It gets lonesome at times."

Sarah seethed, then took a deep breath. "Eli would never love you. And I think it is very sad that you have to kidnap a man just to have company. Perhaps if you weren't so evil, you might be able to attract one the normal way."

"I'm a ghost," Madras said flatly, as if Sarah was stupid.

"That doesn't mean anything. I have heard of many ghostly romances in the clearing where you wanted to build your mansion." Sarah gestured toward the journal, which she had dropped on the floor when Madras startled her. It lay open to an entry where Madras had scrawled her sordid plans for Witchland.

"Can't you do some sort of spell to get her to tell you where Eli is?" Addie suggested.

"Not with light magic," Sarah responded, ignoring the very slight wave of temptation that she felt to take Addie's advice. "I can't make anyone, or anything, do something against his or her will. Only dark magic forces people—or things—to do things they don't want to do."

Addie wagged her tail. "*I could get it out of her. All I have to do is show her my wolf fangs.*"

"Let's try to work this out without embracing our wolfiness," Sarah chided Addie, who wagged her tail in reluctant obedience.

"*I just want to protect you. And my wolf form scared her last time,*" Addie said.

"I'm not a sissy," Madras responded petulantly. "Your wolf veneer hardly fazed me." Then she sneered. "See, Sarah? Dark magic offers you so many opportunities that light magic does not. You could have anything you wanted, including your man back, if you just stepped over to my side."

"Listen." Sarah sighed. "I don't want to negotiate with you, but I want to save Eli."

Madras narrowed her eyes and stepped closer. Sarah fought the urge to step back. While vanquishing Madras in the past had made Sarah less scared of her, Sarah still felt some nervousness about seeing her evil ancestor's face up close. Her centuries of aging showed in the scars, deep frown lines, and various pockmarks on her skin. Unlike Lativia, who still looked thirty and radiant as a ghost, Madras's true colors showed plainly in how she had changed over the years. There was no doubt that she was a monster; snakes writhing in place of her hair would have been only fitting.

Madras stayed still.

"Madras?" Sarah asked.

Suddenly, Madras raised her hand. A flash of green light split out of her palm, aiming toward Sarah's face. Sarah dodged the flash and tried to run behind a rock column. But the spell ricocheted off of the cave wall and bounced toward her, suddenly piercing her skin.

A sickly sensation filled Sarah, making her want to vomit. As she staggered, struggling to recover her balance, she realized that everything around her appeared dim. Then, an uncontrollable urge to tell Madras that she would help her overtook Sarah. *Who cares about the animals? They are just in the way of my noble ancestor Madras's plans. Money is better.*

"Sarah! That isn't you! Snap out of it!" Addie cried. Connected to Sarah's thoughts, she could sense the strange turmoil taking place inside of her person.

Sarah wriggled with revulsion. "That isn't me! I love the animals and the forest!" she shouted at the top of her lungs. Then she shuddered as the possession took over her again. She arched her back, battling it, while an evil voice erupted from her throat, "Go away, Addie! You're a bad dog!"

Addie cowered but did not go away. She knew that this was not Sarah.

Sarah searched with her mind for something she could hold on to when the demonic possession overtook her. She realized that her love for Addie and Eli was the strongest thing she felt. Focusing on it, she felt the love overtake her, filling her with warmth. Then she shut her eyes and was able to separate the evil voice from her own internal voice.

With a huge wave of determination, Sarah broke through the myriad of ugly thoughts clouding her mind and wheeled to face Madras.

Sarah saw Madras sending another flash of green light. "You can't use your dark magic on me!" she screamed. Then she shouted a blocking spell. Suddenly, a huge white shield materialized in front of her and Addie. Madras's dark spell hit the shield and bounced back toward her in several strong rays of gold and white.

"Now I send your energy back to you as light, tenfold!" Sarah cried at the top of her lungs. Her voice echoed in the cavern.

White light engulfed Madras. She looked shocked for a second, then sick with guilt. She began to shrink in size inside her bulky cloak. Though she was a ghost, and therefore naturally pale and translucent, Sarah could see some red returning to her milk-white face. But just as quickly, she regained her monstrous persona and began to chant another longer spell.

Sarah felt her body grow leaden. She glanced down and saw her skin hardening and cracking as a layer of bark grew over it. Her legs were rooted firmly to the spot. With a strange cracking feeling, she could tell roots were shooting out of her legs, growing into the rock beneath. "That's weird. I'm not particularly scared right now," she muttered before hearing Madras say something about trees in Latin. She realized with horror that Madras was acting on the family weakness.

Addie stepped back and whined in fear. "*Sarah, you have to break out of this!*" she cried.

"I am trying," Sarah replied. "But Madras's spell is very strong."

"Try to save your boyfriend now," Madras snickered, walking around Sarah to admire her handiwork. Addie whined at her but hung back, unwilling to disobey her person and act out in violence. "You will stay here and let me train you. Resist all you want. You're not going anywhere."

Suddenly, Sarah thought of an idea. The crows had given her their powers as they became her animal spirit guides. *What would a crow do in this situation?* she mused to herself.

"Don't even bother trying to sweet-talk your way out of this one. I consider you and Lativia one and the same, since she has had you start to take over her place as ruler of Witchland," Madras purred. "This is my chance to finally vanquish my sister and take back what's mine. Don't think for a minute that you can get out of it this time."

A crow would call upon their murder—I mean, their coven, Sarah thought. *And fly. Fly away from danger.*

Sarah tried to shut her eyes, but the wood kept them plastered open. She realized that that was a good thing, because Madras would not realize anything was amiss. With great concentration, she focused on flying, imagining her spirit as a crow soaring through the air and chanting a spell to unlock her body. Then she imagined reaching Lativia and the Leekins and asking for help. Maybe she could also reach Harriet, though she was not sure if Harriet would help or if she was even still in the caves foraging.

Soon, by focusing on lifting upward and flying, she felt a dizzying sensation as her spirit separated from her wooden body and began to spiral up toward the ceiling of the cave. She looked down at Madras, while Addie looked up at her.

"Don't look at me," she told Addie telepathically.

Addie obediently returned her attention to

Madras, who was continuing to circle Sarah, gloating about her supposed victory.

Sarah found that she had no voice in her spirit form. Instead, she had to concentrate on the words of a spell, chanting them as loudly as she could mentally and forcing all of her feelings behind them. Though she did not know a specific spell to break free of her wooden prison, she sensed that anything she said to the effect of becoming herself again would work. With great effort and spiritual might, she made up her first spell:

From these wooden shackles I fly free,
To fend off the evil attacking me!
I am not wood; I am flesh and blood.
So stop these roots growing into the mud.

At first, nothing happened. Sarah felt discouraged as she watched her own body remain rooted in place. Madras was beginning to chant some new spell to make Sarah evil, and Sarah felt worried that maybe her attempt to think like a crow had failed.

But suddenly, as she chanted the spell a second time with even more desperation, she felt something release in her spirit. It was as if a deluge poured from her, soaking her body below in invisible energy.

Suddenly, she saw one of her arms twitch, and then her leg moved slightly. The bark began to lighten.

Sarah felt disoriented as she was rapidly sucked back into her body. She was relieved to find that she could now move her mouth and eyes. Chanting her new spell one final time, she broke free.

Madras jumped back. With a swift raise of her hand, she sent another flash of green energy at Sarah. Sarah rapidly dodged it and sent up another shield. Madras's spell had had even more force behind it this time; the resultant white energy that Sarah's shield deflected back to her was much stronger, as well.

Madras reeled backward. Then she crumpled to the ground and began to wrestle with herself. Her face was very red, and there was more color to her dull, lank hair. "No! No! Lativian magic will not overtake me," she moaned.

Addie immediately lunged over her and pinned her to the ground, gripping her arm with her teeth gently enough to not puncture her ghostly skin. "*Is she in pain?*" Addie asked.

"I think she is so resistant to good and her sister's magic that it feels like pain to her," Sarah said. "It is joy and goodness and love, searing away the evil within her."

"I don't want this!" Madras shrieked.

Sarah stood over Madras. "I can't make you do

anything, Madras. But I can offer some guidance. In the end, good always wins."

Madras cowered away from her, covering her face with her free arm. Sarah softly chanted a spell, and shackles of glowing light began to form around Madras, relieving Addie's duty of holding her in place.

"Oh, please don't shackle me again," Madras sobbed.

"I have to, for my own safety," Sarah said. "These shackles will fade away when I feel that I am safe from you."

Madras shuddered as her form began to shrink. "I—I don't want to hurt anybody," she squeaked finally as she grew smaller and smaller on the cave floor. "I'm not evil—I wasn't always evil."

"I know," Sarah said softly, towering over her.

"I just want what's mine," Madras went on.

"Lativia's legacy is not yours. You have to accept that fact," Sarah told her.

The mention of her sister made Madras prickle visibly. Rage began to suffuse her face again, but the good energy Sarah had returned to her made her calm down. "I just wish I had all of that for myself."

"Then work for it properly. You go about things the wrong way. You must build a following who loves you by treating living things with respect, by being kind and wise, and by protecting the forest, not hurting it,"

Sarah explained, still using the soft yet determined tone. "Build your own legacy. Stop trying to take what Lativia built, and build something else of your very own." Glancing around the cave, Sarah added, "It seems you have a good start here. Maybe you can build on this and create a wonderful empire down here."

"I don't want to stay down here! I want to be above ground!" Madras sobbed.

"Unfortunately, you are banned from Witchland. If you go above ground, it must be somewhere else," Sarah said.

"I want to be unbanned," Madras whined.

"I'm afraid that that can't be done. You have lost our trust in Witchland," Sarah replied.

"How can I redeem myself?" Madras simpered, trying a new tactic.

"You can't while you're like this," Sarah replied. "You have to become good. One way you can start that process is by releasing Eli, wherever you're hiding him."

"He's in a prison you'll never find," Madras replied. "I'm sorry, but I just can't give up that easily. It would make me weak."

"It would make you very strong, actually," Sarah told her. "Please, where is he?"

Madras looked around, and it was clear she was debating whether or not to give up her prisoner.

Sarah's heart sank when she saw Madras's expression darken as she made up her mind. Then Madras laughed savagely, and Sarah shouted her shield spell once again.

"Don't worry, I won't hurt you or your precious dog." Madras sneered. "But I will be back, when I'm stronger. I have ways of gaining strength and power that are more effective than my sister's ways!" With that, she vanished in a poof of dark smoke, and Sarah's shackles fell to the ground, empty, where they began to fade into nothingness.

Sarah groaned. "Great. I swear I almost had her, too."

"I agree. She was almost ready to give Eli up. I think there's some good inside of her, somewhere," Addie agreed.

"I sure hope that is the case. Somewhere under all of those demons she's aligned herself with, there must be a good witch. But the work involved to transform that evil is a huge task." Sarah sighed. "We have to stay focused on finding Eli. Madras said we'd never find him." Feeling discouraged, Sarah began to search for an exit from the chamber that did not involve the rushing river.

"I wish we had a map," Addie whined. *"I don't like this place, and I want to get back up to the ground soon."*

"Addie! You just reminded me!" Sarah gasped.

"*What's that?*" She wagged her tail and panted, pleased that she had been able to help.

"I was going to summon the Leekins for help. Maybe Lativia and the Leekins know about this place! At least, some of the cave system is under Mount Katribus, according to Harriet. It's part of their territory to care for. We can maybe reach them and find out all of the spots where Eli might be."

"*Great idea! Don't let Madras get to your head! Remember you have your whole coven behind you!*" Addie barked joyously.

Sarah did not know how to channel Lativia without going to the ghostly clearing. But she did know that Clover Figcreek, the leader of the Leekins, often communicated with Lativia using a mirror. On a hunch, she approached Madras's mirror and touched it. The image of a youthful Madras was replaced by a clear, deep pool of light.

Sarah focused on the light, imagining Lativia appearing within it. Her skin tickled as her cells remembered her ancestral connection to Lativia. Slowly, Lativia's face appeared in the mirror. Though she bore a striking resemblance to Madras, her face was a pleasure to see, radiating light and health even in her ghostly state.

"Is that my sister's chamber?" Lativia said, peering past Sarah into the ornately decorated room.

"Yes. I just defeated her again." Sarah sighed. At that second, she realized just how exhausted she was.

"It was hard. Sarah turned to wood!" Addie barked behind her.

"I'm all right," Sarah reassured Lativia. "But I'm in the caves under Mount Katribus, and I need help finding Eli. Can the Leekins aid me?"

Lativia groaned. "You must be outside the bounds of Witchland. Probably in the valley behind Mount Katribus, where the Leekins' banishment does not work and the Leekins do not go . . . I knew Madras could not be far."

"She got away," Sarah said apologetically. "Where she went, I don't know."

"The Leekins will have to banish her further, but that entails them working with other fae from other forests, and they don't like to do that." Lativia groaned again. "I heard from the crows that Eli was sucked through the portal. It has grown weak, and I must make a new spell to eliminate that portal altogether."

"Probably a good idea," Sarah agreed.

"I will speak with Clover Figcreek and see how we can help," Lativia finally promised.

"Thank you," Sarah said, but the mirror had already grown dark. Lativia was not one to chitchat.

After musing for a moment on how to escape the cave chamber, Sarah decided that she must use crow magic to make herself, and Addie, fly. She began to focus on the abilities that the crows had given her, which now felt like a part of herself, in order to figure out how to accomplish that.

CHAPTER SIX
CLOVER FIGCREEK

CLOVER FIGCREEK SAT ON HER THRONE OF LING chi mushrooms that were growing on the side of a large fencepost. The rotting wooden fence had once ringed the coven house of Lativia's Wolf Coven, where Lativia had raised her family and hosted witch meetings. In those days, and in the years after when Spellwoods continued to live in the house and maintain its magical aura, Leekins had lived inside and around it, interacting with the family. It was not unusual to see a Leekin stealing bread crumbs from the dining table or flying down to sip tea from someone's cup in the house. That ended when the house was destroyed by witch hunters in the 1930s and Lativia's descendants had moved to the farm that had remained in the family until the death of Beth Spellwood.

Now the house was gone, with only a few

remaining stones from its walls and a historic plaque to commemorate its existence. But the fence remained. The Leekins had built their lavish city around it. Invisible to the human eye, the Leekins bustled about and carried out the tasks of their daily lives amid flower-stalk apartments, grass-blade bridges, and tree castles. They were proud that their city now included Michael Howler's memorial, since they had dearly loved and worked closely with him during his too-brief time as an attorney and advocate in Witchland.

It was now late afternoon, and Clover Figcreek was supervising the teams of Leekins who saw to the watering of the plants and ilex in the forest. Legions of tiny Leekins marched across the ground, carrying acorn shells full of water on their backs, tramping toward their assigned areas of the forest. Other Leekins flew through the air, lugging tiny button mushroom caps of water by their hands. Some marched along blades of grass, the grass only slightly bowing under their weight, while they dragged little carts of water made of dried and curled oak leaves behind them.

Clover Figcreek's brother, Milo Figcreek, was on the other side of the city, overseeing the distribution of dried animal dung and manure throughout the woods. It was a busy time of year, as they had to keep the forest healthy through the early spring. Ensuring that the late snows and freezes would not kill the plants, which were beginning to go dormant for the winter, was a difficult task indeed.

Clover Figcreek wore her acorn crown and a dress sewn from moss. On her feet were pointy-toed slippers cut from the velvety cap of a red-and-white spotted toadstool. At first glance, she did not appear like royalty, but rather like all of the other nut brown and winged creatures moving like ants around her. But the deference with which everyone regarded her proved her status as the leader of all Leekins. She had not inherited the position, but had rather earned it through hard work and protectiveness. Born around the same time as Lativia, Clover Figcreek had had many centuries to become who she was today.

From her throne, she directed Leekins where to go. Most Leekins had assigned areas of certain types of animals or plants that they always tended to, but others were general workers, free to do whatever was required of them. Clover Figcreek was ordering a large group of free workers into groups of four to tend to the sleeping flowers and bushes within Witchland's village limits.

"Starry Moss, please get me some water," Clover Figcreek told the slim, blue-winged Leekin beside her. "I am parched." Her voice was indeed hoarse from giving orders, as well as settling an arduous dispute among some workers earlier. Though being a leader was difficult, Clover Figcreek had not tired of it yet, and was determined to keep her throne and crown as long as she could. There were many others vying for it, but she did not entertain the competition.

"Sure thing, Clover Figcreek!" the Leekin replied cheerfully. She flittered her wings and disappeared, reappearing a few moments later bearing a cup of water fashioned from a small crystal. Only Clover and Milo drank from crystal; everyone else had cups made of acorns, leaves, or other natural materials. "Cold and fresh from the spring, just the way you like it."

"Thank you." Clover Figcreek sipped the water. "I have a raging headache from our feast last night. Too much dandelion wine, I suppose."

All of the workers groaned in commiseration. Leekin feasts were over-the-top occasions, where everyone partied even harder than they worked. It was essential for morale and motivation to keep working hard the rest of the time.

"Anyway, back to work, all of you. You have your assignments." Clover Figcreek watched the free workers take off in flight to sprinkle sleeping magic on the village plants.

Just then, Clover Figcreek got a strange feeling in her gut. It felt like the prickle one gets when hearing their name. Yes, someone was calling her name, but she could not hear anything. "Did you say my name, Starry Moss?" she asked.

"No, I did not, Clover Figcreek," Starry Moss replied brightly.

"I think someone is trying to call me psychically. Perhaps it's Lativia. Or Sarah." Clover Figcreek suddenly flew off toward the top of the fencepost, where a tiny hole in the side of the decayed wood covered with a little red door marked her home. Many of the Leekins lived in the fenceposts, while others lived in the grass or even pine cones scattered about the area. Clover Figcreek had the highest home of them all in order to watch over her city.

From the front of the home below hers, a mother Leekin was teaching her baby how to fly. Baby Leekins often did not start flying until they were at least fifty years old. This one looked at least sixty, and smiled at Clover Figcreek with chubby cheeks. Clover Figcreek smiled back and then chided him, "You should be flying already, little Seamus Redleaf!"

"Hello, Clover Figcreek," the mother hailed her. "Do you want to watch Seamus fly?"

Clover Figcreek nodded her head in acknowledgement. "Later. No time to chat," she said hurriedly, opening her door.

The interior was littered with miscellaneous things —tiny bits of feathers, dried flowers, a bed of tiny moth eggs Clover Figcreek was keeping warm for their hatching in winter, pretty stones and pieces of snail shells and plant matter she found on her forest excursions. On a little table lay her few possessions: a comb made of snail shell, a collection of tiny sand garnets for good luck, painted pine-cone-scale plates, silverware whittled from tiny branches, tiny crystal cups, a wooden tumbler of dandelion milk, and half of a mistletoe berry she was saving for dinner. At the back of her abode was a hole, which led into the rotted-out center of the fencepost; inside it was a hibernating fruit bat. Clover Figcreek took care of the fruit bat while it slept for winter. She also cuddled against its mammalian warmth on particularly frigid nights.

From under her table, Clover Figcreek produced her most precious possession, a sliver of an enchanted mirror. This divining mirror had once belonged to Lativia. After a fight with Madras nearly a century ago, the mirror had shattered. Lativia had given its shards to everyone she needed to stay in contact with. She had given the smallest shard to Clover Figcreek, who was her smallest contact. Clover Figcreek kept it wrapped in leaves and on a bed of moss to protect it.

Clover Figcreek laid the mirror on her table as Starry Moss flew into the little, cluttered house to help her. Clover spread her hands across its cool surface, which began to ripple. Soon, it was filled with Lativia's beautiful face, her red curls floating around the edges of what Clover Figcreek could see.

"Lativia, Lativia, someone is calling me. Is it your little Sarah?" Clover Figcreek inquired.

"Yes, it is Sarah, trying very hard to reach us. She is trapped in the caves below, fighting Madras. And Eli Strongheart is trapped somewhere in the caves, too," Lativia said earnestly. Her ethereal glow almost blinded Clover Figcreek as it increased in the mirror to match her fervor.

"Yes, I noticed the crows around the portal, chattering about him being taken," Clover Figcreek said worriedly. Then she shivered. "She is down in the caves?"

"She is not in the Mount Katribus Caves, but the ones beyond."

Clover Figcreek's dark brown skin began to turn blue, and she began to shake. "Aiiee! Madras may be in the caves under Blackberry Summit. That is beyond our jurisdiction; I could not banish her from there."

Lativia frowned, and there was a strong hint of disappointment in her voice. "If only you played nice with the other faery folk, you could have banished her much farther away. Being allowed to stay so close, she was able to batter the side of the portal until it weakened enough to let her nab Eli. Sooner or later, it will weaken enough to let her cross the threshold and enter our woods again. Death and age have weakened me to the point where I can no longer fight her. It all falls upon Sarah and the other noble people of Witchland. But there is only so much they can do, as well, without running the risk of letting her win."

Clover Figcreek groaned. "It is a pity I could not control exactly where she went. I don't like her being this close. I wish we could control the caves under Blackberry Summit, too."

Lativia shut her eyes in meditation. She opened them a second later. "Sarah is lost, and she is trying to find Eli. You must provide her with a map to travel through those caves."

"I don't know the layout of those caves," Clover Figcreek said despondently.

"But you know who does," Lativia responded, the gravity in her voice growing even deeper. "You know what you must do."

Clover Figcreek and Starry Moss looked at each other with dread. "The Blackberry Hoppers are not known for their friendly disposition to us. All over that issue with our sunflowers invading their valley and hurting their ecosystem twenty years ago. We and our plant life are still banned from there," Clover Figcreek spoke at last.

"You must call a truce and find out the layout of those caves," Lativia said simply. Then she vanished from sight, and the mirror regained its normal reflective surface. As usual, she only gave the barest of instructions and expected Clover Figcreek to fill in the blanks.

Clover Figcreek groaned as she shoved the mirror shard back under her table. "As if I don't have enough to do today!" she exclaimed irritably.

"Shall I fly with you over to Blackberry Summit?" inquired Starry Moss. She looked very small and blue at the moment, as fear gripped her heart.

An innate dislike and fear of the Blackberry Hoppers dwelled within the hearts of all of the Leekins. It was bad enough that the Blackberry Hoppers were heinously ugly; their ugly personalities only made things worse. It had been a long-standing feud between them and the Leekins, and Clover Figcreek was uncertain this emergency would be sufficient to bring about a truce.

"You and my brother Milo will have to come with me and be my protection," Clover Figcreek said.

They found Milo, who was now whittling new water cans out of old acorns, having dispatched the Leekins under his command to nourish the town plants. As Clover Figcreek relayed what Lativia had said, Milo set down his tiny knife and turned blue as he cried, "Aiee! Does she even know what she is asking us to do?"

"Yes, and she doesn't feel at all concerned about

our welfare with those miserable Blackberry Hoppers!" Clover Figcreek cried.

"Oh no, this can't be done! We don't have time for a battle! Autumn preparations are too important!" he replied.

"I thought so myself, but we have our orders," Clover Figcreek responded grimly. "I suppose we must do what she says and hope for the best."

"I only fear the worst," Starry Moss whimpered.

Milo looked from Clover to Starry, then sighed heavily. "I suppose I'll go with you. Maybe if it's just the three of us, they won't challenge us to a battle."

They then began their journey on wing, skimming just above the grasses and brambles of the forest floor. Various birds, squirrels, and chipmunks greeted them with excitement as they passed. The whole forest loved their protectors. Clover Figcreek knew all of the creatures by name. There were too many for most people to remember, but Clover Figcreek's brain was different, made for storing and categorizing information about her forest. After all, Clover Figcreek arguably was the forest personified.

Once over the top of Mount Katribus, past the clearing where the ghosts congregated and Lativia ruled over the spiritual side of Witchland from a ghostly throne, they entered the meadow on the other side. This meadow was a part of their territory, but it was not officially a part of the Witchland Forest. As they flew lower and lower in elevation, they knew they were rapidly approaching unfamiliar land where, sooner or later, they would encounter the Blackberry Hoppers. To humans, there was no distinguishable boundary, but the Hoppers and Leekins were keenly aware of its existence. Very young Leekins were forbidden to play anywhere near the valley, for fear some harm might befall them. Of course, the Blackberry Hoppers had never been particularly violent and had never hurt a young Leekin, but the caution remained as part of the folklore of the Leekins.

Blackberry brambles tangled together at the bottom of the valley, forming the informal barrier separating the two territories. On the other side, the dark forest of Blackberry Summit loomed as the ground swelled toward the summit's top. Blackberry Summit was a smaller mountain than Mount Katribus, but it also squatted over a much more complex and deeper cave system.

Clover Figcreek gingerly landed on a blackberry thorn and sat, her legs dangling over its sharp point. "I guess we will wait here," she said, trying to hide her anxiety in order to avoid scaring her companions.

Milo and Starry Moss settled on other thorns. They had just gotten comfortable when they heard a shrill screech, a banshee battle cry of sorts. The air filled with a flicking sound. Soon, dozens of the Blackberry Hoppers emerged through the blackberry thicket. They were built like Leekins, except they had long back legs, rather like grasshoppers, that they used to hop along at great speeds. They seldom used their wings, but when they did, they filled the air with droning like locusts. They also had large, hard, metallic eyes and strange-colored hair. The Leekins found them ugly. The Blackberry Hoppers thought the same of the Leekins. At the sight of the emerging army, Clover Figcreek, Milo Figcreek, and Starry Moss all exchanged frightened glances and suppressed their skin from turning blue.

"You know you're not welcome past this barrier!" cried the leader, Lily Silverhopper. Her wings and legs were colored like burnished silver, and her copper-colored hair erupted from the top of her head with an exploding poof. "Yet your legs are hanging onto our territory by one millimeter!" She produced a ruler made of a grass stem and held it up to the thorn to indicate how far Clover Figcreek had encroached on her territory.

"I know, and I am sorry," Clover Figcreek said, wringing her hands and turning blue despite her best efforts not to. "But this is an emergency! We have to work together!"

"What emergency could you possibly need us for?"

Lily Silverhopper scoffed. "You didn't seem too willing to help us with the sunflower snafu! That was a *true* emergency."

"We did everything we could to curb the over-growth of those sunflowers," Clover Figcreek replied, dismayed that this decades-old feud still lingered between them. "The sunflowers were being rebellious. They just liked the sun and soil in this valley too much."

"And whose fault was it for bringing them down here?" Lily Silverhopper demanded.

"Listen. I imagine you are aware of Lativia's descendant, Sarah, no?" Milo Figcreek spoke up.

Clover Figcreek shot him a furious look. She hated not being the first to speak on this delicate diplomatic matter. She had not earned her crown by being the last to speak.

"We are aware of her existence," Lily Silverhopper said testily. "She has nothing to do with us. She puts all of her energies into the Witchland Forest, not the Blackberry Summit Forest, so we care nothing about her."

"What happens in our forest always affects your forest, so helping her is in your best interest," Clover Figcreek replied diplomatically before her brother could speak. "She is in trouble in the subterranean part of your territory."

"Where you banished that evil maniac?" Lily Silverhopper said sarcastically. The others behind her raised their voices in unified loathing for Madras.

"You ought to banish her," Clover Figcreek suggested.

"The caves are under the Glowworm Riders' magical jurisdiction, not ours," Lily Silverhopper responded coolly. "And they like Madras just fine because she feeds them!"

"You at least know the geography of the caves, no? Perhaps you can give us a map. Sarah is lost down there, trying to do something noble for our forest, and we need to help her." Clover Figcreek braced herself for whatever Lily Silverhopper's tart reply would be.

Indeed, it was tart. "That sounds like a personal problem." Lily Silverhopper snorted.

"You do realize that if Witchland falls to Madras, so does Blackberry Summit? You also realize that we need Sarah equally, as her environmental work and magical work protects this whole area, not just exclusively our forest? Whatever she is doing down there, she is keeping Madras at bay and our woods protected. It's in your best interest to help her," Clover Figcreek reminded her. "I am very sorry about the sunflowers, but I think we would be stronger if we worked together. We can vanquish Madras and protect our lands much better without this feud between us."

Lily Silverhopper frowned in thought. Then she moved away to confer in whispers with her friends. When she returned, she nodded curtly. "We'll draw you a map. How you plan to get it to Sarah, I don't know."

"I have my ways," Clover Figcreek said.

Lily Silverhopper rolled her eyes. "Oh, yes, you're just so magical." Then she beckoned another Blackberry Hopper to join her as she began to carve a map into the dirt. She first drew a large circle. "This is the main chamber, under your mountain." Then she drew another off of it. "This is the chamber where Madras dwells, all right? Right below where we stand, actually." She then carefully drew another large circle near it and a series of tunnels. "This is another chamber right above it. And here's the tunnel leading to it from the main cavern. Right under it is another tunnel with a rushing river. Sarah better stay away from that river. It might drown her."

Clover Figcreek and Milo memorized the map before profusely thanking the Hoppers.

"You're welcome. You owe us one now," Lily Silverhopper responded.

"Of course," Clover Figcreek said. "You have helped us; now we will help you. I look forward to working together again."

Lily Silverhopper paused, surveying Clover

Figcreek, before she nodded curtly and hopped away, her cohorts springing after her. They laughed among themselves about how hideous the Leekins looked.

Clover Figcreek rolled her eyes. "Then let's go." As they flew back home, she attempted to channel the mental images she had of the map to Sarah. But it felt like Sarah was still lost.

"I think I'll have to use the mirror," she decided, returning to her home in the fencepost.

As she dug the mirror out, Starry Moss looked at her with confusion. "That will only communicate with Lativia, no?"

"Madras has an identical mirror to Lativia. If she is living in a cave chamber, then I suspect that mirror is there, too. Since Sarah is blood to both of them, she will be able to use the mirror." Clover Figcreek began to clear the mirror of negative energies, focusing on the destination she wanted to reach.

"Sarah Spellwood!" A familiar voice filled the cavernous room, echoing eerily.

"Clover Figcreek!" Sarah spun around, holding up the glowing crow feather in an attempt to see where the Leekin was. She knew she could always rely on the Leekins to help her out when she was in a bind.

"Sarah! She's in the mirror!" Addie cried, bounding toward Madras's large scrying mirror.

Sarah ran after her. Sure enough, the mirror was rippling around a wavery image of the Leekin leader. She was in a small room surrounded by tiny wooden Leekin items. Sarah wondered if this might be the mysterious Clover Figcreek's bedroom. She had never gotten such an intimate glance into the lives of the Leekins.

"Clover Figcreek!" she cried. "You heard me!"

"Of course I heard you, though just barely. You're very far away from me."

"I really need a map!" Sarah cried.

"I know that. Now, I need you to close your eyes and see the image I'm sending you telepathically," Clover Figcreek instructed. "It's a map of that cave you're in."

"Thank you!" Sarah was elated that the Leekin had understood her desperate pleas for help. "It's dark in here, and this crow feather doesn't illuminate very far."

"*Crows are useless, except for talking,*" Addie grumbled.

"They're harbingers, remember?" Sarah gently chided her. "That's their entire duty."

"Pay attention," Clover Figcreek said, irritation apparent in her voice. "Now, here is the map."

Sarah shut her eyes and began to see the image Clover Figcreek was sending to her in her mind. It became strong and lucid. She smiled as she recognized where she was, in Madras's chamber, and then she noticed that there was a large vault located above her. *That's probably where Eli is. I was headed up the right tunnel when I heard his voice. I just fell through a hidden hole into the river along the way,* she thought.

Addie woofed in agreement.

"Stay away from the river," Clover Figcreek warned.

Sarah rolled her eyes. "So much for that. We already fell in."

Clover Figcreek narrowed her eyes. "And you didn't drown? My, those Blackberry Hoppers don't know what they're talking about, then! I hope their map is correct."

"We almost did," Sarah admitted. Then she sighed. "Okay, so you say this chamber is directly above us? How am I supposed to get there? The maze of tunnels you're sending me telepathically doesn't really make much sense."

According to the map, there was no other way to the vault save for the river. Sarah began to despair when she recalled a spell that she had been working on lately with her magical mentor, Daisy, which enabled her to teleport herself through solid objects. The spell was extremely difficult and ran the risk of failing at any point, which could have disastrous consequences. She had only practiced it once, on a wall in Daisy's apothecary. Though it had been successful, it was much easier to do on something like a wall than in a cave like this.

"Do you think I can do this?" she asked Addie. "I've only tried that spell with a thin wall, not several feet of solid rock in a cave!"

"*Of course you can!*" Addie said, always Sarah's cheerleader.

Sarah smiled and thanked Clover Figcreek.

"You're welcome. Now I have work to do, so kindly don't make any other rash decisions," Clover Figcreek snipped. "Autumn is too busy!"

The mirror went dark again. Sarah strode to approximately where the center of the vault over her head was. "This makes me nervous, Addie, but you know I love a good challenge. I just pray we don't get stuck in the rocks!" she said.

She closed her eyes and began to chant the spell. Part of the spell involved imagining the solid object before her as room-temperature butter that she could simply glide through like a knife. She did this with the cave ceiling and felt herself start to levitate, and then her head entered the rock like nothing. She saw nothing but rock around her as she passed through, and it disoriented her. Suddenly, the rock felt very, very hard.

"*Sarah!*" Addie cried in horror. "*We're stuck! Your spell stopped working!*"

"I know!" Sarah felt panic setting in when she realized that she and Addie were totally encased in layers and layers of rock. "I lost focus when I saw the rocks passing around us and I forgot to hold the spell in my mind—I lost my power."

"Please do it again! I am getting claustrophobic!" Addie whined in fear. *"This isn't very comfortable, either, being lodged inside a cave wall."*

"I'll get us out of this mess, I promise. I just really hope Eli is actually in this vault, because this spell is hard!"

But when Sarah tried to redo the spell, she found the solidity of the rocks around her and her sense of intense claustrophobia too distracting. She began to seethe in frustration. Finally, she decided that the only way she could do this was by relaxing. She closed her eyes and imagined herself on a beach, gentle waves lapping at her feet. A smile tickled her lips when she imagined Eli next to her, holding a margarita and wearing no shirt. His abs . . .

Anyway. Butter.

Just like that, she and Addie popped through the rocks. They could both feel bruises forming all over their bodies from being encased in solid rock. But Sarah was more preoccupied with finding Eli.

They found themselves standing in another dank cave vault. The glow from Krell's feather illuminated a small natural rock formation shaped like a seat in the very center. Sitting on it, bound in glowing blue magical chains, was Eli. He had managed to work one of his hands free, which held his radio. It looked like the battery had died, as the indicator light was off. Eli looked a bit disheveled, and there was mud on his police uniform, but he was as handsome as ever.

"Sarah!" he shouted. "How did you find me? Did my radio actually go through or something?"

"It's actually a really long story! I'm just relieved I did find you!" Sarah and Addie bounded to him, and Addie licked his free hand in warm greeting. Sarah leaned in and tried to give him a hug. But as soon as her arms hit the glowing blue shackles, she cried out and reeled back.

"Sarah! Are you okay?" both Eli and Addie cried at once.

"Yeah! Those shackles shocked me." She rubbed her arms, which stung as if she had become entangled with a jellyfish. "I guess no hugs until I get you out of these, right?"

"I'm really happy to see you, but honestly, my butt kind of aches from sitting on rock for almost twenty-four hours. Could you unshackle me, please?" Eli begged.

Sarah laughed and began to recite, *"With all my might, I banish these chains into the night!"*

The chains merely flickered eerily but did not disappear. Eli groaned. "I've been here for hours," he gasped, the agony of boredom and vexation plain in his voice.

Perplexed, Sarah searched her mind for another

spell. "I think I need to use an enchantment unbinding spell," she decided.

> *Where there is darkness, let there be light.*
> *Where there is pain, let there be joy.*
> *Love shall take the place of fright,*
> *And no enchantment shall entrap this boy!*

She envisioned the chains fading and unraveling, and Eli standing to hug her.

This time, the chains went dim, but they did not fall off Eli. Sarah repeated the spell, and the chains went dark, yet still remained.

"This is crazy," Sarah muttered.

"*Remember what Madras told us about her magic,*" Addie reminded Sarah.

"That's right! She draws on the powers of many demons to invoke her will!" Sarah gasped. "I have no idea how to even address that. Do you have any ideas, Addie?"

"*No. I sure wish we still had that mirror to commune with Lativia,*" Addie said, the worry thick in her whine.

"Or I wish we had the spellbook," Sarah added.

Suddenly, she got an idea and began to use the Leekin Banishing Spell to get rid of the demon that was helping maintain the chains. *"Star bright, star bright! We banish you tonight!"* she yelled.

There was a sickly yell of dismay somewhere in the darkness beyond the circle of illumination Krell's feather provided. Then the chains suddenly broke at one link and slithered off of Eli like many snakes, dissolving into nothingness on the cave floor. Sarah and Addie glanced at each other, not wanting to consider that there had been one of the demons hiding in the dark all of this time.

"I want out of this place so badly," Eli shouted, jumping off of his rock seat and hurrying toward the dark entrance.

"Yes, let's get out of here before Madras appears! She vanished, and I don't know where she is," Sarah said.

"You saw her?" Eli shuddered. "I haven't seen her, but I have felt her. I keep hearing evil whispering." He shuddered again and blanched. Sarah had never seen him uneasy before.

"She's getting too close to home," Eli went on, shaking his head grimly. "I was checking on the portal when suddenly I saw these black tentacles snaking around me. I couldn't move. Then the portal opened up and she sucked me through. I wound up in this cave, all tied up, and someone whispered in my ear that no one would ever find me because the tunnel that leads here has caved in halfway through and drops into a river. One day, some spelunkers might find my skeleton or something. They left my radio to tease me, I guess. It definitely doesn't work down here."

Sarah and Addie exchanged looks. "I wouldn't just let you rot in a cave," Sarah told him.

Eli suddenly grabbed her and pulled her close, planting a long kiss on her lips. "I—I love you," he said earnestly.

Sarah felt her heart start to beat faster. "I love you, too," she replied. They smiled at each other for a moment.

"*All right, you two, let's go!*" Addie barked sharply. "*There's still Madras to worry about!*"

"I want to know how she managed to get her magic through the portal," Sarah mused as they began to find their way out of the chamber. "She's banned from the woods."

"I think Jenna and the Leekins need to seal it up better," Eli responded. "There's some weakness in the magic, some loophole. You know Madras will find and exploit any loophole she can."

"Unfortunately, yes. Honestly, I thought I had gotten through to her earlier. But I didn't in the end." Sarah sighed sadly. "She's my blood. I just want to be able to consider her my family instead of a nemesis."

Eli placed a comforting hand on Sarah's back. "You

battled her? Are you okay?"

"I'm fine. The battle was difficult, but I got the upper hand. I had to deflect some bad magic from her, and I tried to talk to her, to reason with her. She almost came around, and then she decided to go back to her old ways and simply vanished! I have no idea where she is." Sarah peered forward cautiously in the feeble light from the feather, trying hard not to fall into the river again. The tunnel they were walking in sloped downward, and Sarah felt relieved to know they were heading back to the central chamber.

"Where was she?" Eli asked, feeling along the cave floor with the toe of his boot before taking each step.

"I actually found her home! Where she's been staying all this time!" Sarah said excitedly. She quickly described the resplendent yet creepy abode below.

Eli looked extremely interested. "Can you take me there? I think we should investigate this place."

"No, no, we need to get you home," Sarah protested. "You're probably starving!"

"I could eat, but first, let's check this place out. Can you take me there by magic?" Eli asked.

Sarah and Addie exchanged looks again, then Sarah sighed. "We got stuck in the rocks earlier. It's a scary spell."

"I have full faith in you," Eli replied.

Just hearing that made Sarah's confidence soar.

After all, I did make it through last time, she thought to herself. "Take my hand," she instructed Eli. Clutching Addie's collar with the other hand, she quickly envisioned the cave floor as butter. They slipped through easily this time and plummeted feetfirst into the vault below. They landed with groans of pain. "Not exactly a soft landing," Eli joked.

Eli held her hand as they stood in the cavernous chamber, the roaring of the river's current echoing off the walls. But as Sarah looked around, she was shocked to no longer find Madras's ornate bedroom. "I swear it was right here," she muttered under her breath.

Addie lowered her nose to the ground and wagged her tail. *"Yes, I can smell it, and her spirit. But nothing is here anymore. She moved it!"*

"Where did she go?" Sarah groaned. "I guess she didn't want us coming back here and finding her again."

"Coward." Eli snorted. "I really want to find that ghostly woman and banish her for good. From everywhere. Not just Witchland. Is that possible, to banish someone to outer space or something?"

Sarah laughed. "I get it, but I am not sure if that's allowed in light magic."

"Probably not. Still a nice thought, though," Eli joked.

"We had better get back to Witchland, get some

food in you, and get to work sealing up that portal," Sarah finally said, after futilely searching some more. "We'll use my spell to get to the main cavern, and then we'll take Harriet's way out, if we can find it."

"*Yeah, it was the lighter tunnel!*" Addie volunteered.

"I have to give you a bath when we get home," Sarah told Addie. "You're absolutely coated in mud."

She wagged her tail. "*I love baths! It really clears my aura and . . . you always give me a treat afterward.*"

Suddenly, Sarah gasped. "Do either of you have any idea how long we've been down here?" She fumbled for her phone, only to find the screen was black. She hoped that it wasn't shot from the fall into the river. She had many important contacts on it, including connections from New York that she didn't really talk to anymore, but still didn't want to lose. Many of her old colleagues and friends in New York checked in on her from time to time, and she thought of them affectionately, but they could no longer relate to each other. Sarah's life in Witchland had changed her so much that her friends from New York often remarked, "Wow, you're sure different."

"Way too long." Eli sighed. "Why?"

"My parents! Dinner!" Sarah cried. "I really hope they haven't tried calling me."

"Oh, I completely forgot!" Eli said, slapping his

forehead. "Not that it wasn't important, just—you know—we've had a lot going on."

"It's okay. I forgot, too. We had better hurry out of here." Sarah closed her eyes in concentration and returned them to the tunnel above. With great caution, they managed to circumvent the hole where they had fallen into the river below and make their way into the main chamber.

CHAPTER EIGHT

THE CHAMBER WAS EERILY QUIET. THE MUD MADE a sloshing sound as Sarah, Addie, and Eli crept across it, toward the lightest of the tunnels. Sarah felt watched and hoped that it was only Harriet being nosy.

"Are you getting the heebie-jeebies right now, or is it just me?" Eli finally asked.

"I'm glad you mentioned it. I really feel weird right now," Sarah agreed. She rubbed her arm, where goose-bumps had risen.

"*Me, three,*" Addie yelped.

Suddenly, Sarah thought she detected movement out of the corner of her eye. When she rapidly turned, however, nothing was there. Now feeling especially on edge, Sarah tread forward, more eager than ever to reach the exit.

Another shadowy movement caught her attention on her other side. Addie growled and raised her hackles. "*Something is in here with us, and it's not just a bat or a newt,*" she told Sarah.

"It's not Harriet, either," Sarah whispered. She clutched Eli's hand more tightly and grabbed Addie's collar. "Could it be Madras?"

"We're under Mount Katribus. The Leekins banned her from here," Eli reminded her.

They exchanged glances, and then broke into a run. Though the mud was slippery, they managed to reach the mouth of the tunnel without any serious falls. Just as they attempted to enter the tunnel, the air in front of them turned green and shimmery. They hit the green curtain with a force strong enough to bounce them back. Sarah's hair stood on end. She reached out to touch the curtain and all of the hairs on her arm bent toward it.

"It's like a force field of energy or something," Eli muttered.

Just as he said that, something pitch dark and vaguely humanoid in shape flew down from the cave ceiling. It landed on the muddy floor behind them in a squat and rose, raising its bowed head slowly to reveal its eyes like glowing red embers. The three wheeled around to see what had landed behind them and stared in horror.

"Sarah Spellwood, you think we'll just let you leave so easily?" it said, its voice like many voices hissing at once.

Sarah soon realized why its voice sounded like that as many more such beings began to sprint toward them from the shadows and drop down from the ceiling. She screamed out the shield spell and enveloped Eli, Addie, and herself in a massive white shield just as the demons began to chant a spell together. Their language sounded archaic and demented, and she couldn't understand it, but she knew it was evil. The sense of evil choked her.

The shield deflected the spell, but the demons kept chanting as they circled in closer. Sarah realized that each demon was using its own spell, overwhelming her shield with dark magic, and she worried the shield might weaken. There were at least a dozen of them. Desperate not to turn to wood, she turned into a wolf instead, and Addie followed suit. As she became closer to the ground on her paws, and her eyes adapted better to the light, Krell's feather floated down beside her.

"You were banned from here, Madras." She growled deep in her throat.

"You may have banned Madras, but not all of us!" a demon shouted. "We are friends of Madras, but we are not part of her. We own her, in fact."

"So that's how she got through the portal. It wasn't

her, per se, but you demons, doing your work!" Sarah gasped. *"That all makes sense."*

"Good luck banning all of us from your precious woods," another demon said in a slithery, whispery voice. "We will defeat you and trap you three in these caves forever so you can't keep us out anymore!" All of the demons then continued their onslaught of dark magic.

A crack formed in one part of the shield. Sarah repeated the spell and strengthened it, but it took all of her concentration. Another crack appeared in a different part of the shield, and Addie growled as a demon slid its hand through. Sarah forced the hand out, just as another crack appeared somewhere else.

"Addie, I'm so worried. I can't fight them off forever!" Sarah cried.

Just then, all of the demons formed a ring around the outside of her shield, joined hands, and began to chant in unison. Sarah's shield fractured into hundreds of shards. They began to fall to the ground like glass, sinking into the mud before blinking out.

Cackling deviously, the demons began to advance closer, still holding hands.

Eli clutched Sarah around her shoulders with one arm and Addie with the other. He crouched over the two wolves, trying to use his body as a shield. *"Eli, don't!"* Sarah screamed. *"They will get you first!"*

"No, they won't!" A familiar female voice filled the cave. Sarah glanced around wildly before her eyes landed on Jenna, standing with Lativia's spellbook. Daisy, Margaret, and Hua stood behind her. Jenna opened the book to a spell, and all four women began to chant the words:

Demon be gone.
You are wrong!
Demon be gone.
We are strong.

"Where do you vermin come from?" one of the demons cried. "We just can't seem to get rid of you."

"They're not going anywhere!" Sarah snarled. She broke away from Eli's protective embrace and sat on her haunches as she began to join in the chanting. Addie also joined in, adding her telepathic voice to the powerful magic.

The cave suddenly filled with a burst of golden light, emanating from each of the witches. It pulsed and spread, enveloping the entire cave. Snakes and salamanders scurried away, blinded; the bats on the ceiling rustled, and Sarah briefly worried that this activity might be throwing off their delicate circadian rhythms. She hated allowing human activity to disrupt nature. But defeating the demons was of paramount importance.

The demons cried out in shock at the light that engulfed them. They huddled together, throwing out their own counterspell. But with six light witches using Lativian magic, they did not stand a chance.

As they began to tremble and cry in resistance to the love and light that was being showered upon them, Sarah declared, *"I hereby ban each and every one of you from this entire cave system and the forest of Blackberry Summit! You may not ever step foot on these lands again!"*

The demons all stared at her, their red eyes wide with dismay. Then, as if blasted by a volcano, they shrieked and covered their eyes as waves of white light washed over them and rapidly carried them away. They were swept up in the river and disappeared into its tunnel. Sarah ensured with her mind that they were then pushed out of the cavern at the end of the river and swept far, far away, where they could never enter the above or below territories of Blackberry Summit or Mount Katribus again.

Everyone stood in silent shock as the light of their spell dimmed and the cavern was once again dark. Bats swooped overhead, chirping in terror. *"Please don't be alarmed. You can go back to sleep. We won't disturb you ever again,"* Sarah placated them.

"Are you all right?" Jenna and the other witches rushed over to Sarah, Addie, and Eli.

Sarah returned to her human form while Addie returned to being the beautiful golden-collie mix that she was. Addie wagged her tail gratefully while Sarah threw her arms around each of her friends. "I thought I might've been done for!" she cried.

"A witch can't be without her coven!" Margaret cried.

"You were down here most of the day. I had to come intervene," Jenna said. "I asked the crows where to go and they didn't even move from the tree. So I started to flatter them in the vein of what you were saying to them and they finally flew off and I followed them here."

"You all didn't know about these caves, either?" Sarah asked.

All of the women shook their heads. "A Mount Katribus secret, I suppose," Hua said.

"I think you might need some help after using the crow's spell," Daisy added. "Animals all use different kinds of magic, unique to each species. When a human uses animal magic, there can be . . . side effects. You should come by the apothecary and let me look you over."

Sarah's eyes flew wide as she remembered her dinner with her parents once again. "There's no time!

If we've been down here a long time, then my parents are surely at the house."

"I didn't see anyone when I stopped by to grab Lativia's spellbook," Jenna said, handing Sarah the hefty volume. "But that was an hour ago, give or take."

"I have to get going! I can't thank you guys enough! Can we meet at Javacadabra tomorrow?" Sarah asked.

"Sure," all of the women agreed.

"I really think you're in no state for dinner with your parents," Daisy said with concern. "You really need to come by the apothecary and . . ."

"I can't!" Sarah was already running through the tunnel, which was now clear of its enchanted green static curtain, and Eli and Addie rushed after her.

"What kind of impression am I going to make? I smell like swamp, and I'm all torn up." Eli gasped for breath when they saw light ahead.

"Hopefully we will have some time to shower and get dressed before they arrive," Sarah replied. They reached the crack in the rock Harriet had told them about and clambered out into the woods. Sarah's heart sank when she noticed it was already approaching dusk.

CHAPTER NINE

THEY FOUND THEMSELVES DIRECTLY BEHIND Harriet's hut within the tree line. Harriet was crouched over a cauldron suspended over a fire outside, stirring its contents with a long spoon. She peered at them emerging from the woods, bruised, muddy from the cave, scraped by cave rocks and brambles, and with parts of their clothing torn.

She cackled. "Usually it's the handsome prince who rescues the princess. But I guess this time it was the other way around!"

Eli cringed in embarrassment. "How did you know she rescued me?" he asked.

"I met her down there. Again, it's a long story," Sarah explained. "I'll tell you everything later."

Eli looked perturbed.

"I'm glad you rescued your Prince Charming. Glowworm soup, anyone?" Harriet held up a steaming spoonful.

"I think I'll pass," Eli said, looking revulsed. Then he turned to Sarah. "I honestly didn't even know about the caves."

"I didn't, either." Sarah shrugged.

"Now you two have a place to get some privacy." Harriet winked. "Cave love!"

Both Sarah and Eli shuddered. "I'm certainly never going down there again if I can help it," Eli declared, and Sarah and Addie vehemently agreed.

"Suit yourselves. Means more glowworms for Edgar and me." Harriet shrugged.

Sarah and Eli hastily said goodbye to Harriet and Edgar. Then they jaunted toward Sarah's house, Addie loping alongside them, the heavy book under Sarah's arm.

"It's already evening," Sarah noted, as dusk began to dim the sky and lengthen the shadows. "I really hope we have time to get a shower." She glanced at Eli and noticed that his hair was a tousled mess, and the streak of mud down the side of his face was tinged with blood. "Are you okay?" she gasped, touching the blood gently.

Eli wiped at the bloody mud smear and shrugged.

"I honestly didn't even realize that I was bleeding." Sarah tried to help locate the wound, and they found a tiny scratch near his ear. "I guess it's bleeding more than it hurts," Eli added.

Sarah fumbled with her tangled hair and plucked out a leaf, likely from the tree overhanging the cave exit. But who knew exactly where it could have come from? The entire adventure below seemed like a blur. "We look awful." She groaned. "My parents are going to be so concerned!"

"I really didn't plan on making an impression like this." Eli sighed.

"I know you wouldn't," Sarah told him. "You would have gotten all dressed up."

"I was thinking about wearing my police uniform," he joked. "It would have made a great impression, and you sure do like it."

Sarah giggled. "You look hot in it, that's for sure."

They rounded a corner, and Sarah's heart sank when she saw her mom's blue Subaru in the driveway of her little cottage. "So much for getting ready. And they're already there, waiting! I hope they haven't been waiting long. This is terrible."

"I really hope I can make this up somehow," Eli said anxiously. "I would hate for my girlfriend's parents to dislike me. I'm not a rude guy."

"I know you're not. We're just going to have to come up with a good explanation." Sarah sighed.

Addie let out a happy bark and raced toward Sarah's mom as she clambered out of the driver's seat. She bent down to pet Addie before standing and observing Sarah and Eli. "Well! We pulled in just in time—oh, what happened to you two?"

Sarah's dad clambered out of the other side, joined Sarah's mom, and ran his fingers through his salt-and-pepper hair, pausing over his bald spot as he had always done since it had first formed when Sarah was in middle school. "Sarah, your hair. And you're bleed-ing!" he added to Eli.

"We—uh, we had a cave misadventure," Sarah said. "Let's go inside, shall we?" She forced a smile as her parents gaped at her. She noticed how their eyes fell to the spellbook and she hoped they didn't know what it was, but it was clear her father recognized it by the stern expression on his face.

"I'm Eli Strongheart," Eli said, thrusting his hand out to Sarah's dad.

Sarah's dad looked puzzled as he slowly shook his hand.

"And nice to meet you, ma'am," Eli added, turning to Sarah's mom.

She stared at him, and her eyes widened as she saw how blue his were. "My," she muttered.

"Let me just run upstairs and get ready," Sarah said. She seized Eli's hand, and they hurried into the house. "Please come in!" she called over her shoulder. Once inside, she stashed the spellbook under some papers on her desk.

In a rush, she located her first aid box and began to dab at Eli's scratch. Eli gently took the sponge from her and said, "Let me do it, hun. You just get ready."

Sarah glanced at herself in the mirror and was dismayed at the explosive mess her curly red hair had become. "Caves are not good for hair," she commented, spritzing her locks with a detangler. She attempted to brush it before realizing there was no hope, so she threw it back with a scrunchie. In a mad scramble, she changed, while Eli stole a glance at her.

"Don't look," she admonished him, fighting with the strap of her dress.

"I can't help it," he murmured, slowly peeling his eyes away. "You're so beautiful."

She paused before him and placed a kiss on his lips. Then she placed her fingers over his and lifted the sponge. "Looks like the bleeding has stopped. Let me put some golden-seal that Margaret and Hua gave me to stop bleeding on it and a Band-Aid."

Eli watched her lovingly as she doctored his wound. Then the pair returned to the sitting room downstairs, holding hands.

Addie lay at Sarah's mom's feet. She looked blissful as Sarah's mom scratched behind her ear. Sarah's parents looked at Sarah and Eli, their eyes demanding answers.

"I really hope you're staying safe," her father said first.

"I'm sorry, Mr. Spellwood," Eli said.

"Please." He held up his hand and then smiled warmly. "Call me John."

"And call me Bernice," her mom said.

"Well, great. Our introduction did need a do-over." Eli laughed awkwardly. "Please call me Eli," he added.

Bernice turned to Sarah once again. "I worry about you every day. I mean, what happened to you?" She pointed downward, and Sarah realized that her knees were scraped and bloody where the hem of her dress ended. Then Bernice indicated Addie, whose hair was filthy and matted.

Sarah sighed. "We . . ." She glanced at Eli and then Addie. The idea of lying killed her. But was the truth any better? "We didn't mean to be late or to look like this. We just had to do something important in the caves under the town."

John startled. "Excuse me, the caves?"

"Yes, there are caves under—" Sarah began.

"I know about the caves," her father interrupted.

Sarah blinked at him. "Really? Apparently very few people know about them."

"They sound dangerous. Please tell me you at least were with a guide who knew what he was doing," Bernice said.

"Your Aunt Beth and I used to explore down there," Sarah's father went on. "I assure you, they're not terribly dangerous. I'm more concerned about *why* you were down there." He hunched forward and rubbed his hands together.

"Dad . . ." Sarah began and halted.

"Just ask what you were going to ask, Sarah," he replied.

"Did you ever hear about our ancestor, Madras?" she asked.

His eyes fluttered with fear for a second before he resumed his calm posture. "Of course."

"Who?" Bernice asked. "The name sounds familiar, but . . ."

"It's the spirit of Lativia's sister, who chose an evil path instead of Lativia's good one," John explained patiently. "She continues to haunt this earth."

Bernice's eyes rolled in fear. "That's terrible. Please don't tell me your little cave escapade had anything to do with this Madras."

"Well . . . Madras has been trying especially hard

to get control over this town, despite being banished. And she took Eli last night. I had to rescue him from the caves, where it turns out Madras has been dwelling," Sarah explained.

"I didn't tell her to do that," Eli spoke up immediately.

John sighed and leaned back, rubbing his hands.

"Oh, my God," Bernice exclaimed. "What on earth?"

"Don't worry, Bernie," John said, placing a comforting hand on her shoulder. "It's a family . . . curse, shall we say."

"This is why I agreed with you when you wanted to put all of this magical nonsense behind us! That and the constant questions I got asked when people learned my last name was Spellwood," Bernice cried. "You never told me about Madras," she added sharply.

"I didn't want to scare you. Madras was always after Beth. She would find grifters to come by the farm and terrorize us as kids," John went on. "Our mother always told us to just close our eyes and wish her away. It usually worked. Sometimes, we had to get one of the dogs to defend us when wishing her away wasn't enough."

"I didn't know that," Sarah said, intrigued.

"You are a lot like your Aunt Beth. More powerful,

perhaps. That is why I worried about you taking up magic and moving here. It's not safe, my dear," John finished.

Sarah nodded. "I understand. But . . . Dad, this place is my home. I can feel it in my blood. I'm actually happy here, for once."

"Witchland is a beautiful place, but there are many other beautiful places," Bernice said. "You can't stay here if this—this Madras spirit is tormenting you."

"I can't leave it," Sarah said, her voice full of emotion and tears swirling in her eyes.

"At least give up this witchcraft," her mother begged.

"Mom, I can't. It's who I am," Sarah responded apologetically. She clasped her mother's hands. "I hate to worry you, but I promise you, I have vanquished Madras every time. I am becoming quite powerful."

"Let's talk dinner," John suddenly declared. "I can't think about this anymore."

"John! We can't just eat after hearing this news! I'll be worried Madras might crash in here and attack us at any time," Bernice scolded.

"It's not like that," Sarah and Eli hastily explained.

"Well, then, you should educate me," Bernice replied. She settled into the sofa, clearly making herself comfortable for a long story.

Sarah and Eli took turns relating the past year's events. Sarah had often spoken to her parents on the phone over the past year since moving to Witchland, even admitting to them that she had become a witch, but she had never related anything to worry them. Now it all came out, and she hated the shock and terror that crossed their faces. But then her guilt was replaced with pride when her mom finally told her, "Well. That's my girl, becoming Lativia Spellwood reincarnate in a little over a year."

Her dad stood and hugged her. "I'm just glad you're all right."

"How do you find time for all of this on top of work? You're still an attorney, right?" Bernice stood and crossed over to Sarah's desk, which held many neat stacks of files.

"Of course I'm still an attorney. Witchcraft doesn't pay the bills. I just manage my time well, I guess." Sarah laughed. "Michael taught me that much."

"I loved Michael, that one time I met him at brunch." Bernice sighed. "Such a shame he died."

"You said Michael died in here? On those stairs?" John pointed toward the stairs where Michael had been shoved to his death.

"Yes," Sarah said somberly. She made a mental note to find Michael tomorrow and tell him all about the caves. *Did he know about them?* she wondered.

There was no guessing the depths of Michael's knowledge.

"Well, there's no ghost here, is there? This house feels quite positive." He nodded. This was the first time in years that Sarah had heard him admit to the existence of ghosts. After he had started denying the existence of magic, Sarah had thought he didn't believe in anything paranormal or esoteric. He had often denied the existence of the ghost in their upstate New York home, and he certainly never brought such things up after Aunt Beth died. Sometimes Sarah wondered if her dad was even a Spellwood, as he became immersed in his criminal attorney practice and spent all of his free time reading boring legal volumes in his study. There seemed to be nothing magical at all in the balding and well-dressed middle-aged man before her.

"Actually, he is a ghost, and he visits me almost every day. He likes to help me work and solve cases," Sarah said. Telling her parents all of this made her feel happy and relieved. Full disclosure was seldom in any attorney's best interest, but when it came to family, Sarah hated having secrets.

"Are you still a horrific cook?" Bernice finally joked, addressing her question more to Eli than to Sarah.

Eli made a face. "I try." Sarah laughed. "I'm getting better, aren't I?" she asked Eli, who forced a smile.

"Sure, yeah, sweetie," Eli said through his still strained but loving smile.

Sarah laughed. "We can go eat at Geno's and catch up, okay?" As she pulled on her coat, Addie jumped up, barking happily.

"*Geno's! Feed me some pepperoni!*" she said.

"No pepperoni. It gave you indigestion last time," Sarah reminded her.

"*Pizza?*" Addie tested.

"Maybe a piece of the crust." Sarah winked.

"Don't tell me that dog is like that goat you always talked to," Bernice said, surveying Addie as if searching for signs that she talked.

"She is," Sarah admitted.

"Best dog in the world," Eli added.

"Too bad she can't come," John said.

"Oh, she can," Sarah said. "She's sort of the village dog in many ways. Everyone loves her."

Her parents exchanged surprised glances. Bernice started to unlock her Subaru as they stepped outside, but Sarah urged them to walk with her. "It's not that far, and we can enjoy this nice fall weather," she suggested.

The waitress, Nancy, knew Sarah and Eli well. "Who are these guys?" she asked excitedly.

Sarah introduced her parents.

"It's so nice to meet you guys! So you're genuine

Spellwoods, huh? Wow, did you ever see Lativia's ghost?" Nancy gushed.

John smiled tightly. Being quizzed about his background as a Spellwood was one of his least favorite things.

Over breadsticks dipped in herb-infused olive oil, Sarah's parents asked Eli many questions about his upbringing and his current job as a cop. "And are you . . . ?" Bernice ventured at one point.

"Magical? Sadly, no," Eli said.

"Everyone has magical abilities. They choose whether or not to use them," Sarah reminded him.

"Well, that's not really my forte." He shrugged. "Sarah can do all of the spells for me."

"Be careful," John teased. "Dating a witch is no joke. That's why most of them stay single."

"Dad!" Sarah admonished.

As soon as she said that, she realized that an abnormally large amount of people were streaming into the restaurant. Nancy, who had apparently let it slip that John Spellwood was eating in her section, led them back. "John, there are people here to see you!" Soon, their table was swarmed by Witchlanders, eager to see the man who had grown up in their town.

"You were just a little redheaded boy with freckles, last I saw you! And now you're going gray!" cried an old lady named Hanna.

"Shame about Beth. I miss her every day!" the baker added.

"John! You never visit! You really must stop by!" someone else said.

John and Bernice looked shell-shocked at the crowd. Their peaceful home lives had made them forget how friendly and social Witchland was. "Well, I didn't expect this little reunion," John finally muttered. "I haven't seen any of you people since my sister's memorial!"

"Such a lovely memorial it was," someone said.

"This is so Witchland." Sarah laughed, and Eli nodded in agreement.

Many of the people who visited began to sit around their table for dinner. Nancy and the owner, Geno, joined the tables at everyone's request, ignoring John's protests otherwise. Soon, the restaurant was completely packed, and everyone was dining in the main room, clustered around the table where the Spellwoods and Eli sat. Nancy ran around, a stressed look on her face, until her manager called in two more girls who had the day off. All of the Witchlanders continued to shout over each other to John and Bernice, not letting them continue to get to know Eli. Despite the minor annoyance, the cheer and love in the room was tangible. Addie thoroughly enjoyed all of the pets and table scraps she received.

After a delicious dinner and wine, John indicated to Nancy for the check. She returned a moment later with a smile and said, "Mr. Sandy and his wife actually paid for you, Mr. Spellwood."

"Oh." He laughed. "What a nice surprise." He looked across the room and found the elderly Sandy couple. He raised his hand in gratitude, and they waved back, beaming.

"Perhaps we ought to visit more," Bernice muttered to him. "This place may be odd, but it's your hometown! And it looks like you were dearly missed."

"Perhaps. We have a reason to visit again," John agreed, gesturing toward Sarah. "But let's find somewhere more peaceful, all right? So that we can get to know you, Eli. This wasn't meant to happen."

"It's okay." Eli smiled. But Sarah noticed he had been quiet for most of the dinner. As she looked more closely, she realized he was completely exhausted and struggling to keep his eyes open.

When they finally managed to say goodbye to everyone, they stood in front of the restaurant, trying to decide what to do. Eli's eyelids drooped. "Poor man," Bernice cried. "You look so tired. Perhaps we should let you go!"

"No, no, I still want to visit," Eli said, his voice sounding wan with exhaustion.

"There's always tomorrow. Don't worry, Eli, we already like you," John said, clapping Eli's shoulder.

Eli beamed. "Well, that was my goal," he said happily. "I'm on shift tomorrow, but we can meet for lunch?" he asked.

They all agreed to meet for lunch at Javacadabra. Sarah's parents then headed back to the new bed and breakfast, The Quiet Willow B&B, which Sarah had recommended. The establishment was owned by an eccentric redheaded woman named Malorie Vulpes, who was one of the few people in Witchland Sarah had not met yet. Sarah was pleased to see that they had embraced walking around the beautiful village. *Since living in New York state, Dad has become so reliant on cars, and he needed to be reminded of the outdoors and his beautiful hometown,* Sarah thought as she looked after them with a smile on her face.

With Eli's leaden arm wrapped around her, Sarah led him back to her house. "I really like your parents," he told her sleepily.

"It was cute how awkward you were around them at first." Sarah giggled.

"Oh, was it?" He laughed. "I hate that awkward feeling. I haven't felt that way since high school."

"That's funny, because you really reminded me of a high school boy," Sarah teased.

"That's how much I like you," Eli went on. "I really

wanted to make a good impression. Because I intend to be in your life for a very long time, Sarah Spellwood."

Sarah beamed. She felt as if her heart was radiating visible light out of her body, she was so overjoyed. "Really?"

"Yes, of course. But at the moment, I just want to pass out and sleep for ten years."

Once Eli had passed into a deep slumber, Sarah took a quick shower and tamed her hopelessly wild hair. She then dressed in her warmest clothes and readied herself to return to the woods. "We have work to do. I have to help everyone seal that portal better," she reminded Addie.

"*I'm so tired,*" Addie groaned.

"So am I. But evil never rests," Sarah reminded her.

As they entered the dark woods, Sarah noticed that her face hurt, as if someone was pinching her cheeks together hard. "Hmm, must be the cold," she told Addie, pulling her scarf over her mouth and nose.

Addie led her to the spot where her friends were congregated around the portal, weaving spells to seal it. They had been working tirelessly to both seal and remove the portal from the woods forever so that

Madras and her demons could never reenter. Margaret and Hua were at work with the Leekins, creating a physical barrier by enchanting plants to grow across the portal entrance and to turn hostile to any unwelcome visitors from the other side of it.

"I'm so sorry I had to go," Sarah gushed, running up to the group.

"Don't be sorry! How did dinner go?" Daisy asked.

"Oh, it was pleasant, until the whole town decided to drop in and see my parents." Sarah laughed.

"That's Witchland for ya." Jenna laughed. Then she paused and peered at Sarah's face quizzically. "Um, what's wrong with your face?" She had never been one to sugarcoat things.

But Sarah appreciated her bluntness. "What do you mean, what's wrong with my face?" She felt her face and noticed that something felt off, though she couldn't place what.

"It just looks . . . pinched. Like narrower or something." Jenna looked puzzled as she turned back to reading from Lativia's spellbook, finding spells to add to the many layers the witches were creating to keep Madras's evil out.

"My face *feels* pinched," Sarah said nervously.

Daisy looked at her strangely. "Well, you let us know if you feel anything else strange. I told you that using any sort of animal magic can have some weird residual effects."

"Like pinching my face?" Sarah asked. "That's so weird."

"You never know what might happen. That's why we're not meant to use animal magic or shapeshift into animals we're not supposed to. You remember what happened to Mayor Lewis," Daisy explained.

Sarah shuddered as she recalled Mayor Lewis, with his itchy patches of fur and feverish hungering for raw meat after he took a wolf shapeshifting potion created by Madras. Then she threw herself into the work at hand.

When the witches had exhausted every spell they could think of to seal off the portal, they decided to hurry down to the cave entrance. Staring at the crevice in the rocks that looked so tiny from outside, Sarah felt all of her instincts shrieking at her to run far, far away. The last thing she wanted to do was reenter that dank, claustrophobic cavern and become lost again, with demons or Madras huddling behind any column or in any dark corner, waiting to attack her. "I can't believe so few people know of this place. My dad said he knew about it," Sarah said.

"Some places just aren't meant to be explored by humans," Hua said gently.

The witches began to murmur spells to flood the caves with good energy:

Cave below, land above,
Let us share only love.
Darkness need not harbor evil,
Nor need evil dwell in dark.
All evil must leave,
And this cave must be clean!

They then linked hands and began to chant another spell to seal off the crevice:

Crevice in the rocks, be gone!
May only smoothness exist.
May the way be obscured by mist—

"Hey!" The witches froze when they heard someone yell behind them. They turned to see Harriet running out of her hut, Edgar bobbing frantically on her shoulder.

"What do you think you're doing!" Harriet cried. She stopped near them, out of breath, her black witch's robe swirling around her heels. "Edgar's favorite glow-worms are down there! You can't seal it off!"

"I'm sorry, Harriet," Daisy began.

"Can't Edgar find a new treat?" Margaret

suggested. "We could grow him something special in our garden—"

"*I want glowworms!*" Sarah heard Edgar squawking.

"No!" Harriet cried.

Suddenly, Sarah heard another familiar sound: the "Aieeee!" cry of the Leekins when they felt threatened. She turned to observe a pyramid of Leekins forming at her feet. They had remained in the woods at the site of the portal, ensuring the magic was foolproof, but now they had flown down to the cave entrance. Their skin was turning from brown to blue. Clover Figcreek flew up and landed on top of the pyramid, where her compatriots supported her on their shoulders. All of their wings buzzed in agitation, filling the air with a locust-like whirring.

"The bats need a way out, too, and that's the crevice they use to fly out at night," Clover Figcreek said, anxiously wringing her hands. "If you seal it, you hurt so many bats."

"I see," Sarah said, stunned that she had not thought of that. She had seen the bats in the caves, too. "We can't seal the entrance," she told the other witches, who nodded their heads in agreement.

"But we have to do something," Jenna protested. "Madras and her demons are down there. We saw them with our own eyes, Clover Figcreek."

Clover Figcreek puffed out her chest haughtily, trying to seem bigger than she was. She was not used to being questioned or challenged by anyone. "If you must know, we have that handled."

"How?" Jenna demanded.

"We have our ways," Clover Figcreek responded snippily.

"Just tell us how, please," Sarah demanded. Though she often worked with the Leekins and had even grown fond of them, she still found many of their eccentric nuances irritating.

"We are working with our sworn enemies, the Blackberry Hoppers on Blackberry Summit, to create a ban on Madras and her demons throughout the whole cave system," Clover Figcreek finally admitted with a hint of indignance in her voice. "Any other questions?" Her skin had started to turn brown again, and the other Leekins followed suit as their agitation faded.

"The what Hoppers?" Jenna asked.

Sarah realized that something on the side of her face itched, and her teeth were starting to hurt unbearably. When she passed her hand over her mouth, she discovered it was merging into a point. When she went to scratch the itch on the side of her face, she felt a crust of something—feathers?! Addie barked as she gazed up at her person and realized she was now unrecognizable.

"Daisy," Sarah cried out, her voice sounding like a parrot's squawk. Forming words was difficult and she hated how she sounded.

Everyone turned to look at her and gasped. "Sarah! You're turning into a crow, I think!" Hua gasped.

Harriet suddenly began to guffaw. "Nice new look, Sarah. I'm sure your new beak will go nicely with those Jimmy shoes!"

Edgar joined in the laughter. "*Not my type*," he croaked.

"Sarah, we need to go to the apothecary now," Daisy said urgently. She looked at Clover Figcreek pointedly and said, "I trust you will handle the cave situation, then?"

"Of course," Clover Figcreek replied huffily.

Daisy grabbed Sarah's hand, and they ran to the apothecary. Daisy fumbled with her keys as she unlocked the door.

"So you have an antidote for this?" Sarah asked.

"Not for this affliction specifically. I'll have to concoct one," Daisy replied.

Sarah sat on the cot in Daisy's back room while Daisy rummaged through her herbs and tinctures, consulting various books that she had spread out on her counter. She had a tiny mirror mounted over her sink, and Sarah kept checking it, despairing at the bizarre streaks of black feathers forming across her face and arms and the way her face had made a perfect point. "I'm a horrifying human-crow hybrid," she moaned.

"Some crow's feet, some wormwood," Daisy muttered to herself, adding dashes of powdered herbs to a bowl. "Hold on, Sarah, I'm almost finished. I just have to make sure this concoction will work."

"What a day." Sarah sighed. "I am bone tired."

"It's already a new day," Daisy pointed out. Sarah then noticed the gray light entering the shop through its blinds as dawn began to break.

"I'm not ready for lunch with my parents." Sarah groaned again. "My eyes are literally red from tiredness. And Eli!" she suddenly realized. "He's probably waking up for work soon. He'll wonder where I went."

"I can't work under all of this pressure," Daisy chided her. "Be patient and everything will be fine."

"I do need to work on my patience," Sarah agreed, taking a deep breath. "Nothing I can do will hurry things along."

"*It will all be okay*," Addie assured her. Sarah smiled wanly as she petted Addie's head.

"Everybody will have to understand that you have a higher purpose," Daisy reminded her. Then she smiled and held up the bowl. "Let me mix this with some colloidal silver and some water, and you'll be good to go!"

Sarah nodded and would have grinned if she had a working human mouth. "You are fast!"

Daisy added the liquids and then handed the bowl to Sarah, instructing her to drink. Sarah awkwardly struggled until she found the right angle to sip the liquid through the tip of her beak. The minute the concoction touched Sarah's tongue, she gagged. The bitter, thick taste filled her mouth and left a foul after-taste. "Oh, I hate this," she gasped.

"You have to drink it all," Daisy told her.

Sarah slowly managed to down the bowl of liquid. Daisy took the bowl and started to make more, which she added to an amber bottle. "You'll need to drink this twice a day for four days," she instructed Sarah.

Sarah strode up to the mirror and inspected her face for changes. "Um, Daisy? Are you sure this works? I don't see any difference."

"It will start to work immediately, but it will only fully take effect and return you to fully human form once you finish all of the potion," Daisy answered. "So, sorry to say, but you'll be looking a bit . . . different for a few more days."

"What?" Sarah cried. Her mind flew to her lunch in a few hours, her boyfriend, and the prospective client she was meeting for the first time tomorrow. "I can't look like this for four days!"

"*I still love you,*" Addie told her loyally.

"I'm sorry." Daisy sighed. "That's just how long it takes to unscramble your DNA."

Full of dread for the surely awkward experiences awaiting her due to her appearance, Sarah thanked Daisy and hugged her. Then she marched back to her house, wondering what Eli would say when he saw his girlfriend as part bird.

"I can't stand to see you like this," Sarah's mother remarked fretfully.

Sarah pecked at her sandwich tenderly. It was tough getting used to eating with a beak, and she continually dropped chunks of food onto the wax paper sandwich wrapper. Famished, she was frustrated that she could not simply devour her lunch as she wanted to. "I can't stand being like this," she agreed.

"I think you're still pretty," Eli said, forcing a smile.

"You're sweet, but you're also a liar," Sarah teased him.

"Your Aunt Beth never would have let this happen." John sighed. "She knew how dangerous it was to dabble in animal magic."

"Daisy tried to stop me. She knows the dangers, too." Sarah sighed. "It was the only way I knew to enter the portal. I'll definitely never do this again, though."

John turned to Eli. "You had better appreciate all that my daughter has done for you."

"More than you will ever know," Eli assured him, placing a protective hand over Sarah's.

"Thanks for bringing lunch to my place," Sarah told her parents. "I won't be leaving here for a few days, I'm afraid."

"What about that client you mentioned?" Bernice asked.

"I tried to reschedule, but he couldn't. So . . . I have this." Sarah held up her winter scarf. "Hopefully my beak doesn't poke through it."

"He will run away screaming." John sighed. "Clients don't like unconventional attorneys."

"*What does it feel like, to be a bird? I love chasing birds,*" Addie told her. Part golden retriever, hunting birds was hardwired into Addie's DNA.

"I have this intense urge to fly," Sarah answered out loud so that everyone could understand her strange experience. "But I don't have wings. At least, I don't think so. Eli, are there wings growing out of my back?"

"No, but your arms have what appear to be pin feathers sprouting underneath," he said, trying to be helpful.

Sarah tried to put her new state out of her mind for the duration of her parents' visit. After Eli went back to work, they played a game of Scrabble. "I like Eli,"

Bernice commented, an M in her hand. She was making a concentrated effort not to look at her daughter's face directly.

"You do?" Sarah said happily.

"I do. Certainly more than Jeff, and you know I liked Jeff at first. But he was never right for you," Bernice said.

"He seems like a good young man," John agreed. "He treats you well," he added.

"And he's so handsome," Bernice fawned.

John glanced at her. "Bernie, don't forget your husband is in the room," he joked.

"I'm just saying, he's a dreamboat." She laughed.

"He is," Sarah agreed dreamily. She glanced at her mother, and they both burst into girlish laughter while John shook his head with mock disapproval.

At the conclusion of their game, Sarah suggested a hike, and her parents blithely agreed. With a scarf wrapped loosely over her beak, Sarah took them on a walk on her favorite trail, leading to the Leekin fence. Her father pointed out landmarks he remembered along the way, and he spent a long time at the Leekin fence, gazing upon the old ruins that had once been the Wolf Coven Lodge and the Spellwood family home.

"Do you see the Leekins?" Sarah finally asked him.

"Those little faery things used to pinch Beth and me awake," her father admitted. "No, I don't see any now. I haven't seen them since I was a boy. Are they here?"

"They're all busy tending to the forest right now, so I can't see them," Sarah replied. "But I see them often."

"I saw a faery once, too," Bernice spoke up. She had been quiet for most of the hike, taking in the nature and smiling gently to herself.

"You have?" Sarah was surprised.

"Of course. I saw one in Switzerland, too," she went on. "I went for a ski trip in college. I was dozing off at the hostel where my group was staying when I heard a strange droning sound, like a big fly. I opened my eyes and—there was a faery! It disappeared as soon as I noticed it."

"That wasn't our kind," declared a tiny, shrill voice.

Everyone turned to see a tiny Leekin hovering by Bernice's nose on its wings. Bernice stared, her mouth hanging open.

"Leekins don't live in Switzerland. Just Mount Katribus, and a few places in Scotland and Wales. That faery you saw would be one of our cousins, the air wasps," she went on.

"Oh," was all Bernice could manage.

The tiny Leekin nodded curtly and took off into the trees.

"Well. That's the first time I've seen a Leekin in years. Shall we continue?" John suggested.

Bernice nodded dumbly, and Addie barked.

Near the top of the trail, Bernice let out a scream. Kelvin the wolf appeared through the foliage. Addie barked in joy and loped to him, licking his nose. "*My love!*" she said giddily.

"Don't let her lick him! He might have rabies!" Bernice shouted.

"*Gee, thanks, lady,*" Kelvin replied, though Bernice could not hear him.

"That's her boyfriend." Sarah laughed. "Kelvin. He spends the night in my house quite often, actually, though he is known to disappear for long stretches of time."

"*Hey, a wolf's gotta eat,*" Kelvin replied cavalierly.

"Oh," Bernice said again. Then she shook her head. "Every time I come here, it challenges everything I believe about life."

"That it does," Sarah and her father both agreed.

Saying good night to her parents that evening, before they returned to the bed and breakfast for their last night, Sarah felt sad. "I need to visit more," she told them. "It was so nice seeing you guys."

"We need to visit more," Bernice said, glancing toward the forest and the looming peak of Mount Katribus. "I forgot how much I love it here."

"Yes, we will come more often," John agreed. "It's not always a bad thing to leave your roots . . . but it's not a bad thing to return to them from time to time, either."

Sarah threw her arms around both of her parents. She tried not to bump either of them with her protruding beak as they held her tight.

"Keep taking care of Eli," Bernice told her. "And don't be afraid to let him take care of you."

CHAPTER ELEVEN

"Would you mind removing that scarf so I can see your face? This seems a bit weird," Mr. Hopson said uneasily.

"Sorry, I'm having, uh, a bad acne breakout," Sarah replied to her new client. Though her beak had subsided enough to speak almost normally, she still looked very bizarre.

"That's fine. I've seen acne before." Mr. Hopson laughed. "I have a teenage daughter."

"I really am embarrassed by it." Sarah shook her head. "Sorry."

Mr. Hopson's smile faded. "I have to admit, this whole meeting has been rather off-putting." He glanced around Sarah's modest home. "And I see you live here, right? This is your house?"

"It is." Sarah nodded. Desperate to change the

subject, she turned a page in the real estate contract Mr. Hopson was trying to finalize for the acquisition of an old house in Witchland. "This contract looks sound to me," she said.

"My wife and I wanted to move to a nice place to start fresh. You see, our daughter has been having trouble at school, and we want to get her into a new environment. She has been caught vandalizing the school and starting a fire."

Sarah's eyes widened. *She sounds troubled,* she thought.

He sighed. "But seeing this place—wow! It's just waiting to be turned into something! I really think I could do a lot with this place. I could make it a tourist mecca. I'm interested in acquiring lots of property here for potential development, and you could make a lot of money with me. But I must admit, I don't feel comfortable working with someone who keeps her face covered."

Sarah's hands started to tremble. She set down the file and looked Mr. Hopson directly in the eye. "Witchland is a strange place, and magic is . . . celebrated here. Many people here believe in it. It's not a place open to development and an influx of people. In fact, I think most people would not appreciate it here."

Mr. Hopson rolled his eyes. "I know, I know, Lativia Spellwood and all that business." He laughed condescendingly. "You see, that's where you're wrong. Where you see weirdness, I see potential, because people eat that magic stuff up. It would be easy to make this a witchy tourist destination for people who are into that." Then he glanced at her strangely, an idea sparkling in his eyes. "I'm assuming you're a descendant of some kind to Lativia."

"A direct descendant."

He slapped his thigh enthusiastically. "See? You could become the figurehead of my business and make so much money on your name. Let's see, a ten-ninety partnership, and you'll get rich."

"I'm not interested in capitalizing on my name," Sarah replied crisply. "It is a sacred name that I treat with honor and respect." *And even if I did want to do this, which I most certainly don't, who in their right mind would agree to ten-ninety?* she added to herself.

He only laughed. "How silly. I imagine you believe in that ludicrous mumbo jumbo, then?"

Sarah bit her tongue.

"I don't like him," Addie told her.

"Should I show him my face?" Sarah asked telepathically. She realized this might be a great way to test Mr. Hopson's interest in the town. He reminded her a lot of John Gonforth, and she hated the thought of having another man like that in the town.

"Do it," Addie responded.

"Well? What are you staring at the dog for?" Mr. Hopson challenged. "You're really going to turn down the opportunity of a lifetime?" It was clear now that he was set against Sarah and making fun of her in his mind. The smirk on his face was infuriating.

Sarah slowly unwound the scarf. Though her beak was receding gradually and her feathers were starting to shed, she still looked more fit for a circus than a law office.

Mr. Hopson froze, taking in Sarah's face with growing horror.

"This is called Witchland acne, and it might happen to you if you're not careful," Sarah explained.

Mr. Hopson bolted out of his seat and ran to the door. Glancing back over his shoulder, he shouted, "I'm leaving you a bad review online!" Then he muttered to himself, "Freaks. All of them," as he ran outside.

Sarah and Addie shared a good laugh. Sarah fetched Addie a treat from the kitchen. "Not everyone is meant for this place," Sarah mused.

"*No,*" Addie agreed.

"I think I'll go pay Eli a visit," Sarah said happily.

"*I think I'll go see Kelvin in the woods,*" Addie replied.

The two parted ways at the door. Addie loped off into the woods. Sarah watched her go, smiling. Then she commenced walking to the bakery, where enticing aromas flowed out from the open door. The bakery had over seventy varieties of gourmet coffees and an espresso machine. Had they wanted to, they could have put the town coffee shop, Javacadabra, out of business. The only thing that kept Javacadabra going was its wonderful owners and the deliciousness of its food.

Sarah ordered a dozen pumpkin donuts and old-fashioned donuts with New Hampshire blackberries, then bought espressos for Eli, Jenna, the new operator, and herself, before going on to the police station.

"You're a goddess," Jenna cried when Sarah walked in, handing her an espresso.

"I thought you might like a special treat." Sarah winked.

"How's your, uh, face?" Jenna peered at Sarah, who was still wearing her scarf.

"Improving," Sarah said, offering Jenna a peek.

Jenna laughed. "Well, it is certainly better. How many more days?"

"Three, hopefully," Sarah answered. "Three too long," she added.

Sarah strode to Eli's desk and perched on the corner of it as he went over some paperwork.

"Hi, my love," he said pleasantly, rising to peck her on the forehead. It amazed and delighted Sarah that he had continued to show her the same affection, despite her crow metamorphic affliction. Sometimes he gazed at her beak strangely, but he still treated her like the same old Sarah. She had always known he had a pure heart, but this proved it to her and made her feel better about her face.

"How can you stand looking at me?" she asked.

"Because you are still beautiful, inside and out, and because you are only like this because you saved my life," he replied. Then he rose and helped her out of her coat, handing her one of the pin feathers that had fallen off and poked through the sleeve of her sweater.

"I think I'll save this with Krell's feather as a memento of this adventure—or should I say, misadventure?" Sarah said, turning the black feather over and over in her hands. She had never in a million years imagined being in a situation where she might get to hold one of her own feathers in her hands.

"I wouldn't mind one for my mementos, as well," Eli told her.

She melted at his sweetness and handed him the feather. "I have more falling off that I can save for you. So, anything new?" she said, admiring how he looked in his crisp uniform, with a fresh shower and shave. The scent of his cologne and aftershave made her mouth water.

"Yeah, a watch fob went missing. The man thinks crows took it. Not sure what I'm supposed to do there."

"Crows?" Sarah perked up. "I doubt it was the

crows. But tell me more, please."

Eli described the case. Then he peered at her, cracking a grin. "What, do you know something I don't? Let me guess, you can talk to crows now that they helped you."

"Actually, I can," Sarah admitted. "And I can turn into one now, and not freakishly like this."

Eli shook his head. "Dating a witch is interesting, to say the least."

Sarah flushed happily. "So, shall we go interview him?"

"Oh, uh, we definitely can. I just didn't think you wanted to go out like that." He indicated her scarf-covered face.

She shrugged. "I'll keep it covered."

"Well, let's go." Eli grabbed his coat, and the two joined hands and left the office.

On the walk through the town, Sarah noticed people had their Halloween decorations up and jack-o-lanterns sitting plumply on their porches. "I've been so distracted, I forgot Halloween is next week. I think I'll invite you, Jenna, Margaret, Hua, and Daisy over. We'll hand out candy, bake Halloween-themed goodies, and make apple cider. And, of course, we'll watch *Hocus Pocus*. That's my Halloween tradition," she told Eli.

Eli smiled apologetically. "That sounds so fun, but

Jenna and I won't be able to make it. Halloween is our busiest night, with all of the kids out doing pranks and other mischief. It's always an all-nighter."

"That's okay." Sarah nodded, understanding fully. "Your job keeping this town safe is more important than anything."

"I will definitely stop by for some candy, though," he added.

"Dressed up as a cop?" she joked.

"Actually, we usually dress up." He laughed. "It's the Witchland Police Department tradition."

"Well, I can't wait to see your costume."

"It's always the same, a zombie. I don't get very creative," Eli told her.

They reached Amos McDougal's cabin at the edge of Witchland. A sign in the yard announced pumpkins and squash for sale. Amos was lounging in his rocking chair, sipping coffee and smoking a hand-rolled cigarette. He rose and politely put the cigarette out when he saw Eli and Sarah at his gate. "Well, hello there! C'mon up!" he said in a chipper voice. "Eli. Sarah," he said, shaking their respective hands. He was an older man with white hair and pressed khaki pants. The scent of coffee, cigarette smoke, and Old Spice swirled around him in a great cloud that reminded Sarah nostalgically of her own grandpa, who had passed away when she was only four.

"Amos," Eli said. "We've come to get a little more information about the watch fob. Sarah here is our prime detective."

"Oh, I've heard." Amos winked.

Sarah forced a smile. She didn't appreciate winks from men she didn't know, but she sensed that Amos was only being friendly, in true Witchland spirit.

"So what happened?" Sarah asked Amos.

"Well, I left my granddad's watch fob on the windowsill here while I was fixing a broken trellis. There was a murder of crows squawking in the tree above me. I turned, and the fob was gone. Sneaky devils!"

"Don't call them a murder. They're a clan or a coven," Sarah corrected him, remembering the duty that Krell had tasked her with to clear up the crows' universal image.

Amos peered at her strangely, then shrugged. "Whatever you want to call it, they stole my watch fob!"

"And you didn't see any of them take it?" Sarah asked.

"Well, no, because they're sneaky pests," he replied.

"They're actually very beneficial to the ecosystem," Sarah informed him.

He looked doubtful. "I would believe that if they

didn't steal my granddad's watch fob! That thing went through the war with him!"

"Are you sure it wasn't a person?" Eli added.

"Well, there was no one around!" Amos cried.

Sarah and Eli started to thank Amos for his time, when he asked, "Do you two want some lovely pumpkins? They're on me for the hard work you two do."

"Sure," they both agreed.

Amos beckoned them to follow him around the back of the cabin to the pumpkin patch. Gloriously plump pumpkins of vibrant orange squatted at the ends of their vines. Sarah gasped as she gravitated toward one. "This one!" she said happily, picking it off the vine.

Eli smiled as he watched her. "Pick one for me," he told her.

"You have to pick it," she chided him.

"Okay, that one," he said, pointing at a random pumpkin.

"No, you have to find one that calls to you! You have to look at it and see the face you're going to carve in it. That's why I picked this one," Sarah told him.

Eli laughed and began to walk around the patch as Amos told them about how he grew such nice pumpkins. Eli finally found one. "I think I'll carve this one to look like—"

"It needs to be a surprise," Sarah cut him off.

Eli laughed and shook his head. "You're like a kid about this, and it's cute. Okay, Amos, we'll take these two."

"They're yours! Thanks again! I sure hope you find that fob," Amos said cheerfully as he showed them out.

"Honestly," Eli said as they returned to the police station, "I didn't get to carve pumpkins as a kid. My mom hated the mess. So I don't have much experience with this."

Sarah glanced at him, and her heart fell. "That's terrible. We'll have to make it extra special this year, then."

"I look forward to it."

"We can carve them tonight, after dinner?" Sarah asked Eli. "We can eat at my house, of course. I really hate being out in public like this."

"It's a date." He pecked her on the cheek before returning to his work, carrying his pumpkin under his arm.

Sarah smiled and headed home to bathe Addie, shower, take a nap, and then get ready. She was already planning what she might wear for their date. Definitely some perfume and some dangly earrings, she decided. But nothing she wouldn't mind getting pumpkin pulp all over! She relished the idea of unwinding in her own home with her scarf off.

That evening, Eli met her at her house. He held his hands behind his back.

"What did you get me?" Sarah giggled.

He whipped out a bouquet of orange geraniums, yellow hibiscus, and purple daisies. Sarah gasped. She couldn't remember the last time Jeff had ever brought her flowers; the fact Eli did made her adore him even more. *The man is pure romance*, she thought.

She showed him inside and began searching for a vase to put the bouquet in as he spread newspapers on the floor. "I wasn't sure what to get for the carving part," he said, showing her a little kit he had bought at the grocery store.

"That should work," she agreed.

She located a nice vase and set up the bouquet on her desk, a central location in the house where she would always see it. "When the flowers start to die, I'll press the petals in a dictionary and dry them," she told Eli.

"I'm glad you like it so much." He smiled. "You should have heard the ladies at the flower shop, tittering and asking me questions about you. Our romance is still a hot topic in this town."

Sarah rolled her eyes affectionately. "We haven't had enough action lately, so everyone in town has to gossip about who is dating whom." She sat cross-legged across from Eli on the floor and pulled the kit of pumpkin carving tools open.

"We've had plenty of action." Eli sighed. "I had a nightmare about being down in the cave again."

"Oh, no!" Sarah reached out and placed her hand over his. "That's terrible. I imagine you might have nightmares for a while, then?"

"I hope not. That was genuinely the worst experience of my life. Anyway, let's forget Madras and all of that horror for now and have fun."

"Oh! I forgot!" Sarah sprang up and ran to the microwave, where a cold mug of apple cider sat. She pressed a button to reheat it. "Margaret and Hua made a batch of homemade cider and brought it by. I thought we could enjoy it while we carved pumpkins."

"I love cider," Eli agreed.

For the next few hours, they carved their pumpkins, playfully tossing pulp and seeds at each other. Addie happily licked up some of the pulp that landed on the floor outside of the swath of newspapers. "*Yummy, pumpkins,*" she said. Though they made a spectacular mess, Sarah didn't mind at all.

She finally felt that she was done and said, "Are you ready to see mine?"

"Almost. I have one more thing to do," Eli replied.

With a swoop of his carving knife, he nodded that he was ready.

They turned their pumpkins toward each other at the same moment.

Sarah's jaw fell when she saw his jack-o-lantern. It was clearly her, with her wild curls floating around her face. He had even added little pinpricks for her freckles.

He laughed when he saw hers. "You carved me, too."

They both laughed and kissed as well as Sarah could with her still-sharply-protruding lips. Then they set up their jack-o-lanterns outside with tealight candles and cuddled on the porch, holding mugs of warm cider between their thighs. Sarah didn't even wear her scarf, she felt so comfortable.

"Nice face," Harriet called as she walked by with Edgar on her shoulder.

Sarah groaned and rolled her eyes. "Ignore her," Eli said. "I think you're beautiful and the best person I know."

She squeezed her eyes shut and pulled him close. "I love you, Eli," she murmured.

"I love you, too. Thanks for giving me a special Halloween," he told her.

A FEW DAYS LATER, SARAH WAS SPREADING sunflower seeds in her yard when she heard a familiar croak in the maple tree. She glanced up to see Krell watching her with gratitude in his eyes. Some other crows were hidden further back in the branches, also observing her with their beady black eyes.

"These seeds are for you and your coven," she said. "Sorry I didn't know to continue Michael's tradition, but you are good to go now."

"I'll let my friends know," Krell responded gratefully.

"By the way, that portal doesn't lead to the under-world. It goes to a cave system, that's all," Sarah added.

Krell shuddered. *"That is the underworld! In our legends, crows who go down there never come back."*

"I suppose it's not a good place for a crow. But Edgar likes it down there," Sarah said.

Krell snorted. *"Edgar has his human coddling him."*

"You abandoned him when he was little and injured," Sarah reminded him. She thought about scolding him for abandoning Edgar as a young crow, then realized that the crows probably had a very good survival reason for doing that. Not being a wild creature herself, she knew that she often underestimated how difficult life in the wild could be, especially when contending with humans as apex predators.

Krell told her exactly that. *"We can't let a youngling hold us back. It is too dangerous and consuming to protect little ones. Besides, I think it turned out well for him."* He added the last part with a touch of bitterness.

"Well, your feather sure helped me find my way around down there," Sarah replied gratefully. "But your magic did make me morph into a weird crow thing for a while."

Krell surveyed her. *"You look normal now."*

"Daisy had to give me a potion, and it took four days to work! I am so glad I'm normal now, and so is my boyfriend," Sarah told him.

Krell, eager to change the subject, commented, *"I saw you were hosting a class about us at the high school the other day."*

"Yeah! I hosted a little public information session for local gardeners and farmers about you guys. I hosted it with Margaret and Hua. Over twenty people showed up. The point was that you guys can eat up to forty thousand pest insects in a nesting season, so you actually help rather than hinder farming and gardening. I was trying to get people to stop viewing you guys as pests," Sarah explained with excitement. "I've been doing tons of research on your kind over the past few days, since I don't have any cases to work on currently."

"I know. We were listening through the window. We liked your message." Krell suddenly flew toward Sarah and perched on her shoulder. His substantial weight impressed Sarah. *"We also heard you defend us to that bad man, Amos McDougal! He uses air cannons to keep us away from his pumpkins! He's one of our sworn enemies."*

"He's just trying to protect his farm," Sarah said softly.

"He can do it a different way," Krell said reproachfully.

"I'll talk to him as long as you promise to leave his patch alone," Sarah replied. "There are other sources of food in the woods and here in my garden. Just ask me and I'll feed you guys."

Krell mulled over her words for a second before saying, *"But those pumpkins are so delicious."*

"I'll plant pumpkins for your kind to eat," Sarah offered.

Krell finally agreed. *"That sounds fair enough. We will leave him alone now, but only if he takes down his air cannons. We hate those things!"*

"Did you take his watch fob?" Sarah added gently. "Perhaps because it was shiny, or because you don't like him?"

Krell narrowed his eyes and picked at a loose thread on Sarah's shoulder. *"I know nothing about that."*

"You're sure?" Sarah chided him. "It belonged to his grandfather. It's precious to him."

"Yes, I'm sure," Krell snapped, then flew away, his wings flapping with indignance. The other crows cawed before taking off after their leader as well.

Sarah watched him go before telling Addie, "His response seemed suspicious, didn't it?"

"Very," Addie barked.

She sighed. "I suppose I have to go and find the watch fob, but I don't know where to begin. Let me think on this."

At Javacadabra, Sarah chatted with Susie as she waited for Susie to brew her usual tea latte. Susie's cat, Zeva, gently licked Sarah's hand while staring tauntingly at Addie. Addie ignored her. "*I know you can see me,*" Zeva teased Addie.

"*Don't torment her!*" Sarah warned the cat.

Zeva blinked at her, her beautiful blue eyes striking against her pure white fur. "*Torment? I'm only asking for a simple hello.*"

Sarah rolled her eyes. She had no patience for cat-and-dog drama right now.

"*Zeva, you know better,*" Susie admonished her cat. Like Sarah, Susie possessed the ability to telepathically communicate with animals. Zeva was her familiar, just as Addie was Sarah's.

The bell over the door jangled as an older gentleman entered the establishment. Sarah knew him as Harold, the owner of the hardware store across the street. He ran his fingers through his thinning gray hair as he surveyed the chalk menu. "What are all these things? I can't even pronounce 'em!"

Susie laughed. "Do you just want a regular coffee then, Harold?"

"Is that even available anymore? Anywhere?" Harold responded with a laugh. "Sure. But do you just have regular cream and sugar? None of this fancy vanilla bean mocha latte swirl pumpkin spice stuff."

Susie laughed and directed him to the coffee bar.

"Nothing too fancy over there, though we do have raw cane sugar. It looks like brown sugar, but it's not."

Harold shook his head. "You ladies and your fancy coffee. Almost as bad as the bakery with its twelve billion flavors!" As he filled his mug with coffee, he mentioned, "I still haven't found my pocketknife."

"Oh, no," Susie responded with a groan. "That's heartbreaking. Who would steal it?"

Sarah wheeled to face Harold. "So your pocketknife is missing?"

"Yes, my favorite one. I take that thing with me everywhere. I was cutting some cords in my yard and I set it down. I turned around, and it was gone!" He grunted unhappily.

"Amos McDougal had his watch fob stolen, too, and he thinks it's the crows. I think he's right. Maybe they took your pocketknife, too," Sarah suggested.

Harold raised his eyebrows. "Oh, yeah?"

"They like shiny things," Sarah said.

He shook his head and grunted. "I figured as much. There were a bunch hanging around my trees when my knife went missing. I'm about to get a pellet gun and shoot those things away."

"Please don't do that," Sarah begged. "Crows are actually helpful, not harmful. They kill pests and warn of danger, like fire."

"They bring good luck," added Susie.

"Good luck? Is that why they stole my favorite pocketknife? They're a nuisance," Harold argued.

"I think I can get your knife back. I have an idea," Sarah promised.

Harold looked at her like she was crazy. "How do you plan on doing that? Who knows where they took it? It could be anywhere in the woods."

"I know it means a lot to you. If I get it back for you, please promise me that you won't shoot the crows," Sarah begged.

Harold shrugged, clearly not believing she could retrieve his knife. "You got a deal, little missy." He paid for his coffee and retired to one of the booths in the back, where one of his old-timer buddies was reading the paper. The two began to chat about what menaces to society crows were.

"I'm still trying to do image control for the crows," Sarah informed Susie.

Susie smiled. "I really admire how you advocate for all animals. And you don't even eat them. That's dedication." She laughed. "I happen to still like fish, though I would call myself a pescatarian or part-time vegan."

"I don't have anything against carnivores, but I just can't bring myself to eat meat. I can practically feel the pain of the animal who sacrificed his or her life for my dinner," Sarah responded.

Susie leaned forward and whispered discreetly, "Tell me your plan."

"You won't believe it, but I can turn into a crow now," Sarah replied triumphantly. "Tonight, I'm going undercover."

Susie chuckled. "How on earth did you gain that ability? You just happened to realize you could shapeshift into a crow?"

"No, it's a much longer story, one I will have to tell you later on. But basically, the crows offered me their abilities and protection. I am now aligned with them." Sarah smiled at Susie's gasp of admiration. "I definitely plan on getting that watch fob and that knife back, and giving them a good talking-to, as well. They need to learn that to improve their image, they must behave themselves."

Susie nodded. "But remember, a bird doesn't change its feathers." She moved on to start cleaning her espresso machine.

Sarah mulled over what Susie said as she walked home to prepare for her night undercover with the crows. Shapeshifting into different animals had recently become one of her all-time favorite activities, and she looked forward to this experience. Being a weird crow hybrid for several days had been unsettling and unpleasant, but she knew that was only because of the animal magic she had used. Shapeshifting was one of her abilities, gifted to her by the crows, and she knew there would be no residual effects. She had consulted with Daisy on that when she formed her plan to go undercover with the crows in the forest.

Addie decided to go off into the woods to see Kelvin. She promised not to interfere with Sarah's undercover work, but to stay near, just in case she needed to protect her.

As she bounded off, Sarah changed into warm black clothes so no one would see her and waylay her with chitchat. She slipped a small silver penknife that Michael had left lying around in her pocket. Finally ready, she snuck off toward the trail system that led up into Mount Katribus.

It was not long before she found the massive oak where the crows roosted together for the night. She spotted Krell at the forefront, his feathers ruffled against the settling cold.

"What are you doing out here at this hour, Sarah?" Krell cawed.

"I want to spend a night with you guys," Sarah replied. "As a crow. Just to see what it's like."

All of the crows fell silent and stared at her. One of them finally croaked, *"Why on earth would you want to do that?"*

Worried that they suspected her plot, Sarah shrugged blithely and explained, "I have never experienced life as you birds do: flying, roosting, and regurgitating food for babies." She laughed. "I think if I can experience it, I can understand things from your perspective better, and that will help me advocate for your species."

The crows surveyed her for a moment before rustling back in their tree to confer in squawky mutters. Krell finally returned to the end of his branch and squawked, *"Then shapeshift and try it out. I doubt you will last the night."*

Sarah grinned. "Thanks, Krell." She shut her eyes and focused on her transformation.

Whenever she acquired the ability to shapeshift into a new animal, it became second nature to her. Without being able to explain or fully understand how, she could access the ability. All she had to do was focus on the animal, and then her body would follow suit.

Her skin prickled as it erupted in thick, shiny black feathers. Her hair began to form into feathers as well. Her face hurt as her mouth and nose molded together and stretched to become a curved beak. Her body stretched and shrunk in different directions, and her arms morphed into wings, while her legs became pencil thin. Suddenly, she found herself much closer to the ground than she was used to, and the silver penknife in her pocket fell onto the ground. The intense urge to fly filled her.

Will I even be able to fly without being taught? Baby birds have to learn how, Sarah wondered as she spread her wings. With a little jump, she found herself airborne. *"I can fly!"* she shouted victoriously.

The crows all laughed good-naturedly as she landed on a branch in their tree. They gathered around her to smell her and preen her feathers, admiring how real she actually looked. *"A human couldn't even tell you're human,"* one crow commented as he ran one of Sarah's neck feathers through his beak.

"Thank you," Sarah said proudly. *"It feels good. Different, but good. I love it. I'm even warm. And suddenly I'm craving . . . suet?"*

Krell bobbed up and down. *"We love suet! There's a block in Wanda Neiderstadt's yard."*

Sarah grinned but then realized that leaving the tree now would be folly. It would expose her to all sorts of prey. In her new form, she had new vulnerabilities that she had to consider, for she was sure that anything that happened to her in animal form would also affect her true human form, and she couldn't afford to be attacked or killed as a crow. The sense of danger and fear that animals have to live with every day suddenly dawned on her. It was quite stressful.

"What's that?" another crow asked, indicating the penknife Sarah had dropped on the ground.

"A present I brought for you guys," Sarah replied

happily. *"I know you like shiny things, so I thought you might appreciate that."*

"Thank you," the crow on the ground said. *"My name is Midnight, by the way."*

"Nice to meet you, Midnight," Sarah said, enjoying the raucous caws she was now able to produce instead of human words. They felt good in the back of her throat.

Midnight flew down, took the penknife in her beak, and flew off. Sarah realized she was missing out and flew after the bird.

"Where are you going?" cried Krell. *"It's dark, and you're going to get eaten!"*

"I have to hide this before someone steals it from me," Midnight replied. She flew to a hollow tree stump not far from the oak tree and perched on it. With a delicate dip of her head, she dropped the penknife into the hole at the center.

Sarah landed next to her, feeling vulnerable from predators in the cold, dark woods as dusk gathered. She felt as if many eyes were boring into her. *"Is this where you hide everything?"* she asked.

"I have many hiding places," Midnight replied. *"We crows are scatter hoarders, not larder hoarders like pack rats."*

"Where else do you hide things?" Sarah asked nonchalantly.

Midnight peered at her with suspicion in her sparkly black eyes. *"Why do you want to know?"*

"Because I am not sure this stump is a safe spot. It is awfully exposed. I feel like I'm being watched just perched here. Why don't we find another spot?"

Midnight surveyed her a moment before cawing in agreement. *"Yes, yes, I have a much better spot. It's where I hide my bigger items so they won't be found."* She dipped her beak into the hole and retrieved the penknife. Then she led Sarah through the trees to another place, a pile of rocks near the stream. Carefully, she tucked the penknife among the stones. *"Each stone marks an item,"* she explained gleefully.

"But people like to come through these woods and pick up stones. This is right by the hiking trail, too. Why not a better place?" Sarah suggested.

For the next hour, as darkness fell completely, Midnight led Sarah to each of her hiding spots in the woods. Sarah found something wrong with each one of them, making Midnight move on to the next. Finally, Midnight groaned when Sarah pointed out the vulnerability of the poison ivy plant under which she had tucked the penknife when Sarah claimed the forest service might come through and cut the poison ivy down. *"Sarah, you are so smart! But this is my last hiding place."*

"Your last?" Sarah ran through the others in her

mind, confident she could find them again in the daylight. After all, she spent a lot of time in these woods and had gotten to know them quite well. She had also marked each hiding place discreetly by scratching the dirt in front of it when Midnight wasn't looking with an X.

"Yes," Midnight panted, sounding exasperated. "*I suppose I could make a new hiding place. . . .*"

"*No, no, this one should be fine,*" Sarah said. "*Now I feel like we're in danger, so let's fly back to the tree.*"

Once at the tree, Sarah thanked the crows for the fun evening. "*I really enjoyed seeing life from your perspective. It will help my class so much,*" she told them.

"*We love your class!*" all of the crows cawed, flocking around her. It was clear that they were full of immense gratitude.

"*You are very welcome, and I will keep hosting it. I already got Harold from the hardware store to agree to stop shooting you with pellet guns, and now I just have to work on getting Amos McDougal to stop using air cannons,*" Sarah said.

All of the crows thanked her profusely.

"*Now I am not very comfortable, and I am getting cold,*" she complained.

The crows stared at her, amazed at how sensitive she was to the cold that they weathered every winter without issue. *"It's not even cold! Weakling,"* one of them cracked, and they all laughed.

"I know I'm a weakling." Sarah laughed along. *"But I really need to go to bed. Good night, guys. And thanks again."* She flew down to the ground and shapeshifted back into her human form.

"Good night, Sarah," Krell said, surveying her carefully.

Is it just me, or does he seem suspicious of me? Sarah wondered. She smiled at Krell, hoping everything was all right, before turning to hike back to her house.

Halfway along the trail back home, Addie loped through the brush and brambles to join her, Kelvin at her side. Sarah cloaked Kelvin in an invisibility spell, since people in the village might not take kindly to a wild wolf in their midst, and let him stay with Addie in her dog bed in the house.

Sarah fell asleep, congratulating herself on a plan thoroughly executed.

***

Eli held Sarah's hand as they made their way through the woods, visiting each of the hiding spots. Sarah investigated each one and pulled out countless coins, keys, butter knives, spoons, and shiny bottle caps before returning them to their respective holes.

"These crows are such pack rats." Eli laughed, surveying the various items Sarah produced from each hiding spot.

"Yes, they are." Sarah sighed. "I don't even know what they want with these things. They don't do anything with them; they just like to hoard them. No watch fob or pocketknife yet, though."

"That's okay. I'm quite enjoying this hike with you," Eli said softly, pecking her cheek.

Sarah grew warm as a blush spread across her cheeks. "Me, too," she said happily.

"Can I ask you something?" Eli inquired.

"Of course," Sarah responded.

"What are you looking for? Right now, at this time in your life." It was clear by the traces of strain on his face that this question was difficult for him to ask.

Sarah swallowed as butterflies filled her stomach. "Um, you mean romantically?" she prodded.

He nodded and laughed. "Yes, and in life in general."

"Well, in general, I just want to . . . to be. If that makes sense. I want to keep doing exactly what I'm doing. Learning to be a witch, advocating for animals, defending the forest, and making a little money with real estate clients. Romantically"—she flushed—"I want to be happy with you."

"Thennnnn does that mean you're looking for marriage? Kids, maybe?"

"I am," Sarah replied, her heart beating frantically. "And you?"

"Absolutely." Eli stopped walking and pulled Sarah gently around to look her square in her face. "But I have to take it slow. I need time to . . . get used to this, I guess. It has been a long time since my first marriage, and you know how that ended. I want to be a perfect partner before we start thinking about marriage."

"I am fine with slow, but I think you're already wonderful," Sarah responded. "You don't need to be perfect for me. Just be yourself, the way you have been, and I'll be happy."

"Honestly, I have never met a woman like you. You are fun, funny, smart, athletic, and into some of the strangest stuff." Eli laughed.

Sarah had to laugh in return. "I am a witch, and I guess we're a pretty eccentric bunch."

"You are eccentric, but that's what I love about you. I wouldn't have you any other way than exactly the way you are." Eli swallowed, watching Sarah's face as she melted at his words. "But that's why you deserve me at my best. You know that I have some . . . trust issues, since my ex-wife had an affair."

Sarah nodded. "And I know you struggle with trusting enough to start again. I am honored that you have tried with me."

He grinned. "I didn't think I ever would be able to date again, but that's because I didn't know you existed yet. You blow my mind every day."

"We'll take it slow and keep getting to know each other. And I hope I can continue to blow your mind." Sarah beamed up at him, falling even more in love with his handsome face, something she didn't realize was even possible since she already loved him so much.

Then, to lighten the seriousness of the situation, Eli added, "After all, how many other women out there turn into crows to find old men's antique watch fobs? I think it's really hot that you can turn into different animals and brew potions and go invisible."

"I think everything about you is hot," Sarah admitted, laughing. "The way you protect this town, the way you go to work even when you're dead tired, the way you care about animals and the environment, the way you treat me like I'm the only woman in the world. The way you look in your uniform, and your eyes."

Eli beamed, then looked away self-consciously. "I have trouble taking compliments, but I'll take those ones. Thank you."

"You know I have trouble taking compliments, too, and I have trouble expressing my emotions. You make me want to work on that," Sarah confided in him.

Eli nodded. "I guess we can both help each other grow and work on things."

"That's honestly the kind of relationship I've always wanted, though I didn't even realize it. My ex-husband didn't want me to grow. He resented me for being a great lawyer. But you always support me and make me feel like I can achieve anything."

After smiling at her for a moment, Eli pulled her close and planted a kiss on her lips. Sarah relished the feeling of his lips, his chin stubble, and his tongue as he gently slid it into her mouth. The way his firm back muscles felt under her hands made her want to swoon.

Finally, they broke apart, and she led Eli on to the very last spot Midnight had showed her. She was delightfully flustered from their wonderful conversation as she began to carefully trim back the poison ivy with some garden shears she had brought in her pocket.

"There's my penknife." She laughed, pulling it out.

Eli reached for it. "I can hold it in my pocket if you want."

"No, no, it was my gift to the crows." Sarah peered into the ivy thicket and gasped. "And here they are!" She had to trim a few more leaves back in order to safely reach in.

"Let me do that. I don't want you getting rashes," Eli said, gently pulling her hand away and reaching into the hole she had cleared. He felt around and produced the watch fob and the pocketknife. Rubbing the bit of dirt that had gotten on their shiny silver surfaces, he grinned. "Harold and Amos are going to be happy."

"I just have to come up with a good story about how I found these things. Neither of them will believe the true story," Sarah said.

"You never know." Eli shrugged. "It is Witchland, after all."

"Good to know you used the gift we gave you to trick us," Krell spoke up from the tree overhead.

Sarah jumped and shouted in surprise. She had not even noticed Krell there, and she had even checked the trees at every hiding spot before excavating them. "Krell," she said, guilt tightening her voice. "What—what are you doing here?"

"Midnight may be a juvenile, and therefore naïve around humans, but I have had significant experience with your kind. I knew there was something strange about your visit to our tree and your present last night." Krell shook his head disdainfully. *"Take your penknife back, and don't ever visit our roosting tree again. You are not welcome among the Witchland crows any longer. We also rescind our acceptance of you in our*

clan and our willingness to be your animal spirit guides."

"Krell, wait," Sarah cried despairingly as the bird flapped away.

"What happened? Was he talking to you?" Eli asked. Though he knew Sarah could speak to Addie, he had a hard time getting used to her abilities. He himself could not hear animals speak.

"Yeah, and he feels betrayed. He says I'm not welcome among his kind anymore." Sarah was crestfallen as she put the penknife back in the hiding spot, hoping it might placate Midnight. "I only did this so that I could set a theft right, and also keep the crows from being regarded as nuisances in the town. Harold was talking about shooting them with a pellet gun."

"Oh. That's terrible," Eli said sympathetically, rubbing Sarah's back comfortingly. "Did you explain that to him?"

"No. I should find their roosting tree tonight and tell them the truth." Sarah sighed. "Anyway, let's go back to town and give these things back. I can't let this incident ruin my wonderful hike with you."

Nevertheless, as hard as Sarah tried to stay cheerful as they hiked back down the mountain, she felt terrible.

CHAPTER THIRTEEN

That night, Sarah put on black again and headed to the roosting tree. She was determined to set things right with Krell and the crows.

When she arrived at the tree, however, she was surprised to see that its branches were completely empty. The remnants of old nests, from crows and other birds, hung in disrepair from the bare branches. Sarah groaned. "Where could they be, Addie? Do you hear or smell them?"

"*I smell them everywhere in these woods, but I don't hear them,*" Addie responded apologetically. "*I have no idea where they might be now. But I have a feeling they don't want to be found.*"

"Maybe you can ask Kelvin where they went. Surely he would know, since he lives in the woods and it's hard to miss all of those crows. They have such a huge mur—sorry, a huge congregation. I forgot I'm not supposed to call them 'murders' anymore."

"They'll forgive you for everything, don't worry," Addie assured her. *"They still need you. I'll find out from Kelvin where they are and you can apologize."*

But it turned out that Sarah did not actually need to find the crows.

The next morning, she was woken up at the crack of dawn by a cacophony of raucous cawing and wings flapping outside her window again. Stepping into her slippers. Wrapping her robe around her, Sarah strode up to her bay window and looked down upon the maple tree. "I really hope Eli is okay," she muttered to Addie, who worriedly looked up at her, wagging her tail with anxiety. "They were here to tell me bad news last time, and I'm scared it's more of the same," Sarah went on.

Her maple tree's branches were laden with more crows than she had ever seen in her entire life, so many that the branches bowed down under the weight. The crows looked aggressive and furious as they squawked at her window. Then she noticed the massive splotches of bird droppings all over her porch railings and her Beamer parked out front.

"Oh, no, Addie, what will my clients think?" Sarah groaned. "This is going to be a massive cleanup job. I hope they haven't ruined the paint on my car."

"It looks they have launched several, uh, shall I say poop bombs at your windows downstairs, too," Addie said.

Just then, one of the crows flew overhead and aimed another poop bomb onto Sarah's bay window.

"What on earth is going on?" Margaret and Hua came storming up the drive from their house next door. Margaret was waving her arms, trying to disperse the crows, who only laughed at her and cawed with more aggression. "Sarah!" Margaret called. "Sarah, are you awake?"

Sarah hurried downstairs and admitted the two women through a crack in her front door. She didn't want to open it all of the way and have the crows get droppings into her parlor. Some droppings landed in Hua's hair as the two of them rushed into the house. Sarah brought her a paper towel and began to help her wash it out in the kitchen sink.

"I have never seen so many crows in my life! And why are they messing everywhere? What did you feed them?" Margaret demanded.

"Nothing. I offended them," Sarah said guiltily.

"How did you do that?" Hua laughed as she scrubbed at her neat black bob in the sink. "I don't think I have ever heard of an offended bird."

"Corvidae are eerily intelligent," Margaret commented.

"I sort of tricked them into revealing where they had hidden Harold Whittimoor's favorite pocketknife and Amos McDougal's watch fob. Now they feel betrayed. They became my animal spirit guides, and now they say I abused the gift they gave me." Sarah felt crushed as she related the tale. "Honestly, I see their point, and I feel horrible for what I did."

Margaret placed a comforting hand on Sarah's shoulder. "Sounds like you were only trying to do what's right. Now we need to make them see that."

"I want to do that right now, but I really don't want the crows to aim for me," Sarah said, anxiously glancing at the window.

It looked as if more crows were joining the massive mob already in her tree. They now covered her front yard and perched along her porch railings, as well. The mess was unbelievable, as now they were also throwing dirt and dead feathers at her house with their beaks.

Margaret and Hua exchanged looks and began to laugh.

"It's not funny!" Sarah protested.

"How about you take a white flag and wave it out your front door? Maybe they'll know what it means?" Hua suggested, handing Sarah a white napkin to use for that purpose. "Wave it for a truce and speak your piece."

"Good idea." Sarah accepted the napkin and cautiously opened her door.

"There she is! The traitor!" the crows all jeered.

Sarah stuck her arm out and waved the napkin. "Truce!" she cried. "Please! I have to say something to you all!"

The crows fell silent, one by one. Sarah's ears ached from the noise they had been making. Sarah peeked out, half prepared for another attack, but the crows were still. They stared at her expectantly.

"If you have something to say, then say it," Krell ordered.

The other crows croaked in agreement.

Sarah opened the door the rest of the way and stepped out on the porch. "I must say first that I am terribly sorry. I had only the best intentions for you all. I tricked you because you wouldn't give up the watch fob and—"

The crows began to caw and bounce around on their feet angrily once again. *"It's all about greed!"* they shouted. *"Humans have millions of possessions and they can't let a single one go!"*

"No! Harold was going to start shooting you guys with a pellet gun! It might kill some of you! And that was Amos's grandfather's watch fob. It meant a lot to him. You must understand that stealing things only makes people think of you as nuisances and pests, which is partly why you have a bad image," Sarah shouted over the cacophony.

The crows fell silent again as Krell yelled at them to cease. He flew and landed at Sarah's feet, cocking his head so that he could look directly at her. *"Are you saying it is our fault that you humans misunderstand us?"* His eyes held a challenge.

"Not your fault entirely. We certainly could do better at educating ourselves. But you don't help matters any, and you could improve your image exponentially if you stopped stealing and eating people's gardens." Sarah shrugged.

Some of the crows started to hop up and down in anger, but Krell told them to be quiet. He mulled over what Sarah said before finally asking, *"Then why didn't you just say that? Was there really a need for the subterfuge?"*

"There wasn't," Sarah admitted. "That's what I feel so ghastly about."

"We don't steal much. Especially not things that people use," Midnight added. *"It's not worth shooting us over."*

Other crows raised their voices in agreement.

"No, it's not worth shooting you over. But Harold loved that knife. And to Amos, that fob was a family heirloom with priceless sentimental value to him. And I happen to know that you guys have also been eating from the gardens of the local farmers. People need this produce to sell; it's how they make a living. When I went through your hiding holes, I found lots of keys. Who knows how many people got locked out of their houses or cars because you stole their keys? Locksmiths are not cheap," Sarah explained desperately. She really hoped the crows would not take offense and launch an even worse attack on her now.

Addie came out and sat next to Sarah. "*And Sarah said she and Eli found lots of coins. People need their pocket change at the store,*" she added helpfully.

Sarah sighed. "See? Stealing anything is not good, guys."

Krell observed Sarah and Addie for a few moments. Then he said, "*Excuse me while I confer with my coven.*" He flew into the tree, and the crows gathered around him, muttering among themselves.

After what seemed to be an agonizingly long time, Krell finally flew back down to Sarah's feet. "*Okay, we conferred, and we understand your reasoning. We agree to stop stealing things that people need, in order to protect ourselves.*"

"That's wonderful," Sarah said elatedly. "Now, do you accept my apology?"

Krell peered at her thoughtfully, then excused himself again. After another extremely long conference in the tree, he returned to her feet and bobbed his head in what Sarah realized was a nod. *"We decided that we will forgive you. We will continue to be your animal spirit guide and welcome you among our kind. But it is only because you have done us a favor. We still do not appreciate what you did, but we must admit that it was something we probably would have done ourselves had our roles been reversed."*

Sarah nodded graciously. "Thank you. I am honored to have the crow as one of my animal spirit guides."

"Now will you help us clean up this mess?" Addie barked.

For the next few hours, the crows and their magic assisted Sarah, Margaret, Hua, and Addie with cleaning up. When the house looked like itself again, the crows said goodbye and flew off into the trees.

"We have to go eat," Margaret told Sarah, giving her a hug.

Hua also hugged her. "That was interesting, to say the least. The things that happen in Witchland!"

"No kidding." Sarah laughed. Though the afternoon was a bit chilly, she had broken a sweat scrubbing crow droppings off of her car.

Once Margaret and Hua were gone, Sarah retired to her rocking chair in front of her living room window. She gazed out at the maple tree and the yard with its bare flower beds, awaiting the springtime that was coming soon. She imagined worms wriggling beneath the earth and beetles starting to tunnel upward for another summer of hard work.

"For spells' sake, Addie." She sighed. "Let's sum up the past few days, shall we? I saved Eli, defeated Madras again, banished Madras again, gained the crows as one of my spirit guides, shapeshifted into a crow, and solved a theft. Anything I'm leaving out?"

"You encouraged a new alliance between the Leekins and the Blackberry Hoppers, putting a decades-long feud to bed," Addie said helpfully. *"And you helped save the crows from being shot by Harold Whittimoor."*

Sarah grinned. "And I opened a conversation about marriage with the man of my dreams." She began to scratch Addie behind her ears. "I must say, I enjoy being a witch. And I am getting pretty darn good at it."

Addie licked her hand in affectionate agreement.

CHAPTER FOURTEEN

AT THE HIGH SCHOOL, SARAH SET UP BOARDS WITH pictures of crows tending to their young and other such tender acts in hopes that people might relate to crows better. She turned to smile as people began to shuffle into the classroom where she had been allowed to host her second crow education class.

The first person to enter was Amos McDougal. The watch fob Sarah had returned to him glinted from its place on his belt. "Well, hello, Miss Spellwood." He smiled and winked. "I heard about your movement to ban shooting crows and air cannons in this town, and I thought I'd come on by and offer my two cents."

"Your opinion is welcome, but I do hope my presentation can change your mind about your stance," Sarah said warmly. After dropping off the watch fob with Amos, she had requested that he stop using air cannons, but he had met that request with stubbornness.

"I don't think it will. You see, I don't think you have a right to make a town ordinance like that. Some of us need our gardens to grow food; some of us need it for making a living," Amos replied. He was still being polite, but Sarah could see how agitated he felt.

"I understand," Sarah began.

Just then, Mrs. Roth entered. She looked angry as she set her purse on a desktop. "I'd like to know who appointed you queen of this town," she said sharply. "Making an ordinance like this! My eggs are my living now, and those crows scare my chickens!"

A steady stream of farmers, gardeners, winemakers, and chicken keepers entered the room after Mrs. Roth, raising their voices in protest of the movement Sarah was spearheading.

Sarah sighed and sat down on her chair in front of the audience. "I understand that the crows are a nuisance," she said. "But we Witchlanders love nature, and we love our land. We don't like to hurt things."

"We don't, but sometimes we have to," everyone agreed.

"Not in this case. Crows are very intelligent, and they can be trained." Sarah turned and started her presentation, skipping ahead to the part where she outlined a plan to train the crows to stay away. "Using a system of cues, we can train the crows to leave our gardens alone. But we must also feed the crows, or they'll continue to eat our produce," Sarah explained. "From now on, the village will set out sunflower seeds and grow a special garden just for the crows."

Her presentation was met with thoughtful silence. Finally, Mrs. Roth asked suspiciously, "And who's going to pay for all of this food and the garden?"

"Well, I think we can all contribute a few dollars now and then to the fund," Sarah replied. "Can we vote on this?"

People slowly nodded and raised their hands. "It's worth a shot," they all agreed.

"I want them to stop stealing our stuff, though," Amos spoke up.

"Crows like shiny things, but they are also vindictive," Sarah explained. "If you stop shooting them and using air cannons, they will probably stop stealing your sentimental possessions. We can offer them shiny things we don't want by placing them in their special garden."

The meeting concluded with people discussing details and planning where the community crow garden would go. They hiked out past the high school and chose a spot on village property. Sarah marked it with rocks and vowed to come with Margaret and Hua the next day to start the plants in the cold. Only with their magic could they make things grow in the freezing dirt.

"I hope this works," Mrs. Roth said testily.

"If it doesn't, then I will repeal the ordinance," Sarah promised her. "But I know it will work. I've done a lot of research, and I know a lot about crows. They just want to peacefully coexist with us, really."

She nodded curtly and hobbled off toward her chicken farm.

"Thanks again for getting this back to me," Amos said, holding up the watch fob. "It is more precious than you know."

"I know." Sarah smiled, patting his shoulder affectionately.

"Here's a few bucks for the food and garden fund," Harold Whittimoor said, handing Sarah a wad of ones. "My store sells the seeds, by the way."

"We'll be sure to buy the seeds then and support your business," Sarah said brightly.

He smiled and winked before heading on home.

"*What a success,*" Addie said.

"*I agree.*"

Sarah glanced up to see Krell talking from the pine near the prospective garden. "*I enjoy having a good food supply for the winter. It's the hardest season for us,"* he went on.

Sarah beamed. "I am glad I could help you guys. And thanks for upholding your end of the bargain. I haven't heard any complaints about you lately."

"Of course," Krell cawed and flew off, looking quite happy.

Pleased at how the meeting had gone, Sarah returned home to get things ready for the little witchy Halloween party she was hosting with her friends. She put on spooky music and began to bake candy corn bars using a recipe she had found online.

As she put on mascara in her bathroom, she realized the house was growing hazy and she could smell burning. She rushed back into the kitchen and pulled out the bars to find them burned to a crisp.

"I can never cook, and I apparently can't bake, either." She sighed, tossing the treats into the trash.

"You can order stuff from the bakery or Java-cadabra," Addie said helpfully. *"It's still open."*

Sarah groaned. "I just wanted to bake something original this time, but you're right." She and Addie hastily jogged to the coffee shop, where they got the last of some autumn leaf-shaped cookies and some pumpkin cheese muffins. "At least I know these will be good," Sarah told Addie with a self-deprecating laugh. "I don't know what

I was thinking, subjecting my friends to my baking."

"*I like the treats you bake me,*" Addie said kindly.

"Dogs just like more . . . varied foods than humans." Sarah laughed.

Back home, Sarah finished getting ready just as soon as her doorbell rang. All of her coven sisters were standing on the porch. Sarah hugged them and ushered them inside. She put in her rather worn *Hocus Pocus* disc and began making popcorn and setting out the treats around the couch.

The doorbell rang, and Sarah gave candy to the group of little trick-or-treaters outside. She smiled as she closed the door. This was her first Halloween in Witchland; she had been too busy during the first one to do anything special or give out candy. It felt good to do that, since there had been no trick-or-treating in her upscale neighborhood in New York. In fact, there had hardly been any kids in her building.

"So nice to enjoy Halloween," Margaret said happily. "No Madras to worry about."

"That portal is sealed for good, and the caves are cleansed," Daisy agreed. "And Sarah is a human again!" Everyone giggled, including Sarah.

The doorbell rang again, and Sarah opened it to see a very handsome zombie on her porch. "Well, hello."

She giggled as Eli wrapped his arm around her waist and pulled her against him.

"Hi, my love," he said, kissing her and smearing some green face paint on her chin.

Sarah laughed and wiped off the makeup. "Thanks for popping by. We just started *Hocus Pocus*."

"Of course." Eli poked his head through the door to greet Sarah's coven sisters. "Well, I have a serious toilet paper situation at the high school to contend with. The kids apparently wrapped the trees, parts of the building, and anything they could. But I had to see my beautiful princess. That's what you're going as, right, a beautiful princess?" he teased.

Sarah laughed. "If that's what you see," she teased back.

Eli pecked her on the lips and left. Sarah shut the door and sat down, heart fluttering with happiness. "I'm going to marry that man someday and live out the rest of my years in this town. I love it here so much," she said.

Curious to find out what happens when the town's luck is stolen and Sarah can't find the culprit?

Get Impawsible Mischief Now
http://getbook.at/impawsiblemischief

A NOTE FROM MELANIE

Ms. Addie Pants loves to snuggle with her mom.
She also loves crows and talks to them often.

Thanks so much for reading this book. I love how the light and magic of the crows help Sarah and Addie solve the crime at hand. Don't you?

This story was special to me as I worked with crows in a rehabilitation facility during graduate school. Their intelligence is humbling and I never took it for granted. Everyday I would spend time feeding and talking to them. I was enlightened by their wisdom.

But lynx, wolves, and crows are not the only spirit animals for Sarah to discover. Check out the next book and I can't wait for you to hear about their next journey.

Stay tuned for a sneak preview of the fourth book in the series, *Impawsible Mischief*, which is now available on Amazon.

http://getbook.at/impawsiblemischief

Thanks again!

Paws Truly,
    Melanie Snow and Addie

PS: Reviews help authors keep writing. Please feel free to leave one!

Impawsible Mischief
The Spellwood Witches, Book 4

Stolen charms. A mysterious woman running for mayor. Can beginner's magic save an ill-fated land?

Novice witch Sarah Spellwood wants to grow her powers and protect her village. But to win over a cunning fox familiar who can improve her gifts, she must learn who's behind Witchland's missing good luck. And when the small community's misfortunes multiply, she's in a race against time to save the residents from themselves.

As accusations fly, Sarah is shocked to discover a greedy poacher hunts her would-be spirit guide. And with tensions already bubbling over, the witchy wolf-shifter and her talking dog Addie have to sniff out the answers before the quaint little town is doomed.

Can Sarah stop the disaster from spreading before her home suffers a terrible fate?

Impawsible Mischief is the magical third novel in the Spellwood Witches cozy mystery series. If you like wisecracking creatures, enchanting characters, and close-knit sisterhoods, then you'll love Melanie Snow's clever story.

Buy Impawsible Mischief to cast out evil and mayhem today! http://getbook.at/impawsiblemischief

ENJOY AN EXCERPT FROM
IMPAWSIBLE MISCHIEF

Do you want to find out if Sarah can stop a disaster from spreading in Witchland before her home suffers a terrible fate? Can can one witch and her furry pal stop misfortune from turning into a catastrophe? You will be able to find out in the next book of the series: Impawsible Mischief!

Impawsible Mischief is now available on Amazon. http://getbook.at/impawsiblemischief.

Download your copy right now! You're not ready to get your own copy? Enjoy part of the first chapter for free on the next page!

Impawsible Mischief

Chapter 1

Impawsible Mischief, Book 4 of The Spellwood Witches

"It's such a nice day," Sarah Spellwood said, happily breathing in the rich fragrance of flowers that had permeated Witchland's atmosphere.

The first green shoots had started to break through the ground and dust the trees, and now Hua's gardens and the town's gardens were erupting in full bloom. Witchland always blossomed earlier than anywhere else in New Hampshire, Hua had explained to her, largely thanks to the Leekins, the small faeries populating the woods and spreading their plant magic to keep the area verdant. Their spells caused the crocuses to spring up through the snow in startling shocks of green as early as January sometimes.

"It was a bit of a rough winter," Hua replied, also pausing to enjoy the fresh late April weather.

Sarah knew that Hua was not just referring to the cold and weather, but also to the evil that had threatened to topple Witchland last November—Madras Spellwood, Sarah's ancestor and sister to the powerful witch Lativia. Madras had turned to dark magic while alive, and now her evil ghost kept threatening to take over the forest and town of Witchland, both of which Lativia protected.

Sarah's golden collie mix and familiar, Addie, could tell Sarah was thinking of Madras. She looked at Sarah mournfully and barked, wagging her tail in sympathy.

"It sure was," Sarah agreed with a shudder. "I'm incredibly happy Madras is gone for good. It seems everyone wants to take over this bit of paradise, but we have a great little army."

"We sure do." Hua winked. The army Sarah was referring to was composed of local witches, of which Sarah was one.

A familiar cackle brought Sarah abruptly out of her reflections on the past November. "That one is crooked!" Harriet taunted from across the street, where she was walking by with her crow, Edgar, perched on her shoulder.

Sarah rolled her eyes and surveyed the flyer. It

looked perfectly straight. She realized that Harriet was only taunting her.

"Can't see through all that mascara, huh?" Harriet continued to cackle as she walked away.

"I'm not even wearing makeup!" Sarah shouted after her.

"Don't let her bother you. She likes you; that's why she teases you." Hua laughed.

"No time to waste with banter!" Harriet shouted back without looking behind her. "I have lost my lucky bauble, and I won't be right until I find it!"

"Lucky bauble?" Sarah shook her head, watching Harriet's receding back. Then she surveyed the flyers she held in her hand. They urged people to attend the mayoral debate at the town hall tomorrow, part of the election process to replace the former mayor, who was now in prison for murdering the town clerk and stealing the town deed, which had held Lativia's protective spell against Madras. It had taken the town government some time to recover from Mayor Lewis's theft and arrest, and its acting mayor, Susan Lake, had decided that she did not want to become the official mayor. As a result, elections for a new mayor were just now taking place. "I printed four hundred on recycled paper, and so far we've put up eighty. Think we've put up enough?"

"Of course! I can't imagine anyone in this town

doesn't know I'm running yet, after how hard we've campaigned," Hua said. Then she sighed. "Let's go back to my house and take a break."

Sarah followed Hua back to her lovely house, which was surrounded by gorgeous gardens just beginning to sprout. In the back, a barn converted into a greenhouse stood, and Sarah knew it was brimming with verdant plants inside. The sweet odor of churned manure with newspaper and composted food waste hovered over the place, mingling with the sharp scent of the chilly air and Margaret and Hua's woodstove smoke billowing from their chimney. This place always felt like home to Sarah, as much as her own home and the coffee shop in town where she spent a lot of her time.

Hua sighed, lowering herself into a rocker. She was neither old nor overweight, but a certain exhaustion had begun to overtake her lately. "I really just can't wait for all of this to be over, honestly." She groaned, rubbing her eyes. "Too much work! Too many meetings! And all of the planning! Now we just walked all over town and put up eighty flyers."

"There are still three hundred and twenty left." Sarah laughed. "Maybe I printed too many."

"Maybe?" Margaret teased, entering the covered porch. "I know you're exhausted, honey," she went on, handing her wife a steaming mug of fragrant tea. "This is a tea to revitalize you."

Hua beamed and puckered her lips at Margaret in a kissing gesture. "I couldn't have made it this far without you. And you," she added, including Sarah with a glance. "I think I would be in the hospital with a heart attack by now otherwise."

"All this work will be worth it in the end," Sarah reassured Hua.

"Speaking of worth it, I have to show you a new plant I acquired. It cost us an arm and a leg to order it through a seller online, but it was definitely worth it." Hua's eyes lit up the way they always did when she spoke about her two deepest passions: agronomy and plant magic. "Let's go back to the greenhouse."

"You're in for a real treat!" Margaret declared, rubbing her hands together with excitement.

Sarah followed the two herbal witches into their packed, humid greenhouse. She always wondered how the women could find specific plants among the seemingly countless species packed onto the tables and shelves, growing every which way, even through the winter.

"This baby is the Echinoflava interrupta," Hua said proudly, holding up the pot of a small, red prickly-looking plant with a single yellow flower sprouting on top.

"What does it do?" Sarah asked.

"Do you have your cell phone on you?" Margaret asked. She was beaming, as was Hua; the two clearly anticipated that Sarah would be stunned by whatever the plant could do to her phone.

Sarah produced her phone from her back pocket.

"Hold it up to the plant. See what happens," Hua urged.

Sarah did as she was instructed. Instantly, her screen went fuzzy and then black. She tried to turn it back on, but it would not work. "Oh, no," she cried in dismay.

"Now go stand a few feet away," Hua instructed.

Sarah hurried away from the plant and breathed in relief as her phone finally turned back on. She had too many important contacts and pictures on that phone to lose it all to some electronic-interfering plant.

"It blocks all electronics! Literally scrambles their electromagnetic energy so that they can't work!" Margaret crowed.

Hua clapped her hands exuberantly. "And this baby . . ." She led Sarah on to another strange-looking dark fern. "This one is like a catnip for foxes. As you know, we are going through a period where our foxes are dying because of distemper introduced by feral dogs, and this plant could help."

"We should plant it everywhere," Sarah exclaimed.

"Not so fast. We have to test it first, to make sure it won't disrupt the ecosystem here," Margaret informed her.

"Now take this plant, for instance. This one is drawn to metal," Margaret went on, leading Sarah deeper into the greenery of the building. She showed how the vines of the plant curled desperately, almost greedily, around a metal stake. Then she held a penny up to the plant. Rapidly, a leaf unfurled, grew toward the penny, curled around it, and then snatched it and retreated to hold the coin close to its stem.

"We call it the greedy morning glory," Hua announced. "Very rare, from the Japanese island of Kyushu. People there think it's evil and try to eradicate it."

"Another part of our job as witches is keeping these species alive, ensuring they are not destroyed," Margaret added.

Sarah gently touched the leaves of the plant and felt a vague, warm energy emanating from it. "Yeah, it's not a bad-spirited plant," she agreed. She knew what bad spirits felt like now, quite well.

"I want to try something with you. I want you to tell me what a plant can do by scanning it," Hua declared.

Sarah thought of Michael Howler in his wolf form, still eager to help her communicate with ghosts, plants, and animals. Michael had been her mentor in law school and after she landed her first job at a real estate law firm; however, she had had no idea he was a powerful warlock until she moved to Witchland and spoke to his ghost atop Mount Katribus. Now he was also her mentor in magic, just as the other witches in Witchland were. After she had inherited his law practice in Witchland, where he had spent his last years, she had solved his murder and put his killer behind bars for life. Now she took care of his dog, Addie, and continued his work advocating for the protection of the Witchland Forest from human activities, such as development and poaching. No matter what, she was not alone.

"Um, how do I begin?" she asked, as Hua and Margaret led her to a nondescript, nonflowering plant growing near their robust, colorful tomatoes.

"First, clear your mind," Hua instructed her.

Sarah began to clear her mind, a difficult task that she had become increasingly good at.

"Now, reach out to the plant. It can be helpful to envision your mind as a hand. When you touch the plant, you will feel him touch you back, and then he will speak to you," Margaret went on.

After a few frustrating failures, Sarah started to imagine the strange day in the forest when she had first heard Addie speak. She vividly remembered her shock, and her fear that she was losing her mind. Then she remembered how she came to know Addie as a sentient being with a voice. It turned out that all beings had such a voice and full consciousness, far more than most people guessed. This plant had a mind and spirit and, thus, something to say. Focusing on that knowledge, she felt herself start to stretch beyond her frame, out of her skin. She felt herself brush against the plant, even though she was not physically touching it.

Only then did her mind fill with a pleasant, clear male voice with a cadence much like a wind chime. *"Hello there,"* it said.

Sarah took a startled step backward. *"Why, hello,"* she replied, glancing at her mentors, who were smiling.

"I'm Nipkin," the plant said.

"I'm Sarah. Pleased to meet you. What do you . . . do, Nipkin?" she asked.

"What do I do?" He paused. Before Sarah could clarify what she had meant, he began to sing, *"I grow tall and lean! And the sun shines down on me, down on me. The birds peck at me, oh, they peck at me, and I know I'll be back in spring. From a little seed, a little seed, I spring, and the caterpillars inch along me!"*

"Do you feed the birds?" Sarah inquired. *"That's your purpose, feeding birds?"*

"And caterpillars and worms and things! I feed, I feed, I feed. Things grow from me." Nipkin seemed

quite content with himself as Sarah thanked him for speaking with her. *"Oh, of course!"* he sang. *"I like speaking to things, to the living beings, to the things that feed on me, on me."*

"I suppose he's . . . he's a food plant?" Sarah told Hua and Margaret, unsure how to clearly describe what Nipkin had just told her about himself.

"He is a type of milkweed that is almost extinct due to a nearly complete loss of habitat. He is very critical to his ecosystem," Margaret said proudly. "Even the simplest plants matter immensely in the big picture."

Sarah glanced back at Nipkin, his sweet spirit tugging at her heartstrings. She felt a tear form in her eye.

Hua and Margaret clapped their hands, beaming. "That is today's lesson!" Hua declared, pleased with Sarah's pupilage.

GET YOUR COPY NOW
To Finish Chapter 1
http://getbook.at/impawsiblemischief

DISCOVER
THE SPELLWOOD WITCHES SERIES

WITCH'S TAIL, BOOK 1

Can she awaken her dormant powers and stop a desperate killer destroying the forest? If you like paranormal puzzles, delightful canine companions, and environmental enlightenment, then you'll love Melanie Snow's wagging-ly fun whodunit.

Here's the link to buy the book today!
http://getbook.at/witchstail

HOWL PLAY, BOOK 2

A novice witch. A collie companion. Can this clever duo put noses to the ground to chase down a killer? If you like cute flirty romance, discovering one's true destiny, and love for animals, then you'll adore Melanie Snow's barking-ly fun adventure.

Here's the link to buy the book today!
https://getbook.at/howlplay

TAIL OF A FEATHER, BOOK 3

A mysterious portal. Eight crows with a message. A missing police chief. If you like paranormal puzzles, charming canine companions, and a bit of flirty romance, then you will love Melanie Snow's crafty quest. Take flight into the magical world of Witchland.

Here's the link to buy the book today!
http://getbook.at/tailofafeather

IMPAWSIBLE MISCHIEF, BOOK 4

Stolen charms. A mysterious woman running for mayor. Can beginner's magic save an ill-fated land? If you like wisecracking creatures, enchanting characters, and close-knit sisterhoods, then you'll love Melanie Snow's clever story.

Here's the link to buy the book today
http://getbook.at/impawsiblemischief

PAWTRAYAL, BOOK 5

When a ghost cries murder, an unsolved case could cost her future. Can this witch solve the magical mystery when an old enemy starts casting chaos. If you like wise familiars, heartthrob romances, and mystical whodunits, then you'll love Melanie Snow's paranormal brainteaser.

Here's the link to buy the book today!
http://getbook.at/pawtrayal

Don't Miss Your Free Gift!

Thank you for purchasing *Tail of a Feather, The Spellwood Witches, Book* 3. To show my appreciation and because of a popular request from my readers I am offering a:

Welcome to Witchland Map
https://wendyvandepoll.com/melaniesnowgift

Join Melanie Snow's Paranormal Cozy Mystery Facebook Group

The Wolf Coven
https://www.facebook.com/
groups/melaniesnowcozymysteries

About Melanie Snow

Melanie Snow is the pen name for Wendy Van de Poll, a bestselling author, pet loss grief coach, and animal medium. She is the author of The Spellwood Witches, a paranormal cozy mystery series.

Her books weave together positive magic, snarky forest faeries, and insightful animals with fun and eclectic humor. True life adventures and intuition are woven into her stories laced with unbridled imagination.

She has been followed by wild wolves in minus sixty degrees, hissed at by a mama bobcat, and played ball with a wild owl—among other animal encounters.

Find out more about her work by visiting her on her at https://wendyvandepoll.com/melanie-snow.

Also get *The Welcome to Witchland Map*.

Download Your Free Gift

https://wendyvandepoll.com/melaniesnowgift

HOW TO FIND MELANIE SNOW

www.wendyvandepoll.com/melanie-snow

www.facebook.com/melaniesnow.cozymysteries

www.instagram.com/melaniesnow.cozymysteries

www.facebook.com/groups/melaniesnowcozymysteries

www.amazon.com/author/melaniesnow

www.goodreads.com/melaniesnowcozymysteries

ACKNOWLEDGMENTS

I would like to thank my intuitive writing team who has guided me to write this fun series. They weren't always easy to deal with but they were patient with my fumbling. Because of them Melanie Snow and all the characters in my head have come to life.

I appreciate all my teachers of the furred, feathered, and finned variety who continue to guide me through life and teach me what matters.

A special thanks goes to my weekly writing buddies H.R. Hobbs and Toni Crowe who are kind, sassy, and amazing authors.

I offer a tremendous amount of appreciation to my beta readers: Nadine, Vicky, and Renee. To my editor

Robyn Margaret Verdugo a huge thank you for your expertise. And thank you to my talented proofreader Allison Rose.

A huge hug goes to my husband, Rick Van de Poll. He is a remarkable poet and human being who dedicates his life to the animals and the environment. He inspires my soul. You can find his books on Amazon, as well.

And of course, Addie. This rescue puppy flew on a jet plane from Texas to grace my life in many ways and writing books with her as a main character is just one. Addie even has her own series called; The Adventures of Ms. Addie Pants on Amazon.